THE GUIN SAGA

Book Four: Prisoner of the Lagon

K A O R U   K U R I M O T O

TRANSLATED BY ALEXANDER O. SMITH

WITH ELYE J. ALEXANDER

VERTICAL.

Published by Vertical, Inc., New York.

Originally published in Japanese as *Ragon no Ryoshu* by Hayakawa Shobo, Tokyo, 1980.

ISBN 978-1-934287-19-4

Manufactured in the United States of America

First Edition

Vertical, Inc.
1185 Avenue of the Americas 32nd Floor
New York, NY 10036
www.vertical-inc.com

And so the terror of battle overran the wide plain, filling it with outcry, white death and red flame unleashed from the very hands of the gods. Then it was that the men and horses saw a phantom, a black harbinger of disaster approaching from the twilight star. Mounted upon a great war-steed it came, a figure of violence incarnate.

—From the *Nospherus Saga* scrolls

CONTENTS

Chapter One

THE BATTLE OF NOSPHERUS

[CONTINUED]

— I —

"We have been…"

The night that enveloped the battered, beaten, and exhausted soldiers left them doubtful of their own hands and features, so thick was its inky veil.

"We have been wrong about a few things…"

Sentries paced endlessly back and forth, their footfalls crackling like dry whispers. Orders were for the lights to be kept low, and all men were to remain in full armor with their weapons at the ready.

At every clang of sword guard against armor, every low whinny of a horse or murmur of conversation at camp's edge, soldiers started and gripped the hilts of their own blades. Their nerves were horribly strained, sharpened to fine, trembling points, and it seemed the lightest fall of a feather could break the silence that surrounded them.

At times the wind picked up and carried strange howls and

cries from far across the sands, grating on the men's taut nerves. Perhaps these howls came from the legendary desert wolves of Nospherus, said to roam a thousand tads a day, or perhaps it was due to the bustle of some other, more foul creature of the Marches desert.

It was a night of terror. The Mongauli army, wounded and restive, felt vulnerable, and the merciless denizens of Nospherus hounded them without pause. Drawn by the stench of blood they came: bigeaters, mouths-of-the-desert, sand worms, soundless swarms of vampire moss and blood-sucking flies, even the sand leeches. The disgusting, misshapen creatures shone with sickly phosphorescence as they gave the Mongauli no end of nightmares both real and imagined.

Though the giant sand worm and bigeater were indeed frightful, the lesser perils that dogged the Gohrans gave them worse grief. The insatiable vampire moss and flies attached themselves to any exposed skin and dug in so deep it seemed nothing would get them out, and the men were constantly picking tenacious little blood-suckers off of their comrades.

The sand leeches were, like the yidoh, semi-translucent as though all pigment had been sucked out of them, but their hides were covered in bumps sickeningly reminiscent of chicken skin. When these leeches or the tight whorls of vampire moss attached themselves to human flesh, they sucked up blood until their swelling forms were a breathtaking crimson. When a victim finally peeled off the stuff and stomped on it, what seemed an impossible amount of blood gushed out and seeped into the dry, gray sands.

Had any one of them—the ten and five thousand elites culled from the five knightly orders, the pride of Mongaul—expected a mere five thousand wildlings to wreak such havoc on their expeditionary force? The troops had crossed the black river Kes, the boundary that separated the desert marches from eastern Gohra, hoping to see Nospherus swept clean of Sem through their valor and transformed into the newest domain of glorious Mongaul. Leading the fifteen thousand: Lady Amnelis of the golden mane, the archduke's daughter, who at only eighteen years of age was General of the Right. The aides who rode out with her: the diviner Gajus Runecaster and the white knights Feldrik, Lindrot, and Vlon. Loyal to her followed Count Marus, lord of Tauride Castle, and his two thousand blue knights; from Talos, two thousand black knights and Captains Irrim and Tangard; and under the divided command of the young viscounts Leegan and Astrias, two thousand red knights from Alvon. With twenty hundred crossbowmen and roughly five thousand footmen supporting the knights, Amnelis's army should have been unstoppable.

Mongaul was in need of a victory. The three archduchies of

Yulania, Kumn, and Mongaul, which made up the Gohran Alliance, a new force in the Middle Country, maneuvered endlessly amongst themselves to maintain their delicate balance of power even as they attempted to expand further into that plain where reigned such formidable rivals as Parros, Cheironia, Earlgos, and Kaulos. It was Mongaul that had made a surprise attack on the elegant kingdom of Parros, which ages of peace had lulled into a sense of security. Yet, ironically, by taking the famed crystal city into its hands, Mongaul had endangered its position within the Gohran Alliance. Fearing that Archduke Vlad of Mongaul was growing too strong, indeed strong enough to threaten their own sovereignty, the Archdukes Olu Khan of Yulania and Tario of Kumn seemed to be entering into a secret pact to oppose Mongaul.

Nor had the conquered kingdom been as great a boon as Vlad had hoped it would be. Although Parros was now under Mongauli rule, the supporters of the High King Aldross's orphaned twins, Prince Remus and Princess Rinda, who had miraculously escaped the flames of war, were ceaseless in their resistance of the Mongauli occupation.

Thus, it must have seemed bizarre indeed to any stranger's eye when Mongaul suddenly turned its attention from its newfound prize in the Middle Country to the barren wildlands of Nospherus. Yet the change in strategy, unexpected though it was, was no act of madness. The Golden Scorpion Palace of Mongaul had become aware of a great secret that lay in these wastes, and Archduke Vlad had decided that sending Amnelis and a full invasion army after it was a critical step towards the realization of his ultimate ambitions.

But now, in the wake of three violent encounters with the wildling Sem tribes, the Mongauli army was reeling from the shock of defeat, and, although it had not been driven from Nospherus entirely, it had been forced to retreat and regroup.

Their numbers remained strong. The gravest damage that had been dealt to the invaders was psychological. The redoubtable Captain Leegan and his vanguard had been engulfed and devoured by a swarm of yidoh, but when the dust settled it became clear that the actual number of soldiers that the seething monsters had transformed into ghastly lumps of melting flesh was not great. Though the loss was painful, the yidoh-ambush had fallen short of a decisive blow. Later, the Sem tribes had attacked twice under cover of night, overrunning the outer pickets and sending ripples of fear through the main body of the troops, then fading as swiftly as they had appeared. Yet, including the dead and wounded from these two raids, the number that Mongaul had lost that day was no more than three thousand by the reports; even when these deaths were added to their earlier casualties, the Mongauli army was left with over ten thousand largely unscathed troops. The invading force was still more than twice the size of the combined army of all the Sem tribes.

Nonetheless, the faces of the Mongauli troops that turned to one another when the orders to camp for the night were finally given were filled with defeat and despair. The attacks had taken their toll.

Dominance in numbers does not always mean a dominance in spirit. In fact, the Gohrans, while they still retained an over-all advantage, had been reduced by a greater proportion of their power than had the Sem; they had lost nearly a third of their original fifteen thousand while the wildlings had lost only a fifth of their five thousand. The invaders felt their loss weigh more heavily with every report of a casualty that came in during the night.

The warrior Guin could have told them why they were beaten, why they had tasted, and not just once, the bitterness of defeat. He knew what made them tremble like the remnants of a routed host even though they remained superior in numbers: it was Nospherus. The Mongauli were in enemy territory. They had stepped over the border, out of human lands, and now it seemed as though the forbidden desert itself had turned its will against them and that all the creatures of the sand had risen in alliance with the Sem to drive them out. The unexpected attack of the horrific yidoh might not have claimed as many lives as at first the Mongauli had feared, but it had devastated their confidence. Now the soldiers jumped at every whisper of the wind or sudden slip of sand upon the dunes, fearing that these might signal the approach of some new terror. Their enemy was Nospherus, and its harsh expanse surrounded them on all sides, and its unrelenting sky spread above them, dark and heavy with menace.

Their thoughts betrayed them, filling them with so great an unease that no matter how often their captains reassured them, telling them of their strength and the certainty of ultimate victory, the soldiers remained resolute in their grimness. Not a few of them cursed the commanders that had dreamed up this ill-omened expedition and their own bad fortune in being a part of it. Under their breath they muttered hopes that the Lady Amnelis would just sound the general retreat and be done with this folly.

There was one thing above all others that weighed upon their minds and left a tangible feeling of dread that they could not shake. The giant silhouette they had seen, looking down on them as the sun set, had cast its shadow into their hearts and made their blackest thoughts blacker still. It was the leopard-headed warrior who led four of the great Sem tribes—the Raku, Tubai, Rasa, and Guro—and their allies from lesser tribes. On a giant black charger he had ridden down the dunes at the head of the wildling army with eyes that blazed yellow as balefires. He was an unknown, a warrior whose very nature was shrouded in mystery, but his war-making had been without equal upon that battlefield.

If they had faced only the Sem tribes, the Mongauli armies surely would not have been driven to this defensive stance. But there was some power in that leopard-headed half-beast that made those he faced quaver and turn aside, their swords and arrows reduced from instruments of death to the unwieldy tools of a terrified defense. He was the embodiment of fear that should not have had form. In their hearts, the soldiers felt the unease of the sacrilegious, as though they took aim at Ruah Sungod or the half-beast god Cirenos himself. They had lost faith that their side was in the right, and an army that doubts its very purpose has already lost.

None of them knew whence came the unease that gripped them when they saw the leopard-headed warrior, nor could they have said for certain whether he truly was man or god as he descended upon them like a storm, leading the wildling Sem to battle, only to disappear into the dunes once more at the battle's end. So it was that during that dark night, which seemed to them all the darker because they were forbidden to light even the customary watchfires, that the soldiers whispered to one another, wondering just who the strange warrior was. But no sooner would a man speak than an anxious officer nearby would scold him.

"Shh! The enemy will hear you!"

And so the soldiers fell silent. But there were some among them who felt a more compelling reason than mere orders not to speak of the leopard-headed one. They crossed their fingers and made the sign of Janos for warding off demons and whispered in hushed voices that none must speak of "him."

"Say not a word... He's no man of flesh like us, he's a demon! Aye, could be Doal Demongod himself come down to earth! And, if he is—"

"If he is...?"

"Then you're best off not saying nothing of him, lest you say something you can't take back. Speak the name of a demon, and you might's well invite him over for supper!"

"Doalspit! Nospherus this may be, but *him*? Here? I think—"

"Don't do it! Don't talk about *him*, I say—may Janos protect us."

"Janos protect us. Say, Doremugh, you were always good at the bettin' table."

"What of it?"

"What do you reckon our chances of gettin' back to Talos Keep alive be?"

The soldier Doremugh's answer was cut off by a shrill command. "Shh! Quiet over there! Did you not hear your orders, you gutter-rats?"

The tone of the voice made it clear that the officer who spoke was just as nervous as his men. The group of footsoldiers dispersed, and the obsidian darkness that surrounded them was quiet once more.

Whether it passed their lips or not, the name of Guin was at that moment the thing most feared by every soldier in the Mongauli expeditionary force. Nor was it the rank and file alone who were so enthralled by the terror of the leopard-man—the mysterious warrior had provoked the curiosity of even the highest commanders.

"It seems we have slightly underestimated the Sem..." General Amnelis addressed her officers, who had gathered for an emergency council in her pavilion. Count Marus, Irrim, Tangard, Astrias, Gajus, Vlon, and Lindrot huddled around the light of a stunted candle already half-burned to the table. "In our current situation, we have no choice but to revise the goals of this operation. We can no longer search for Gur Nuu. It is imperative that we first eradicate the Sem tribes. We will find the hidden valley and build a Mongauli stronghold there only after the eradication campaign is complete. Agreed?"

"As you wish."

"We will do as my lady directs."

"I have no objection to this plan."

One by one, the leaders of the Mongauli army quietly muttered their approval, but there was little spirit left in them.

More than the turn of the battle, it was the loss of Leegan, beloved son of Count Ricard, keep-lord of Alvon, that had made their hearts sink and wrapped them in veils of sorrow.

"Very well. The Sem shall die. And yet—it seems that, above all, we fight not the Sem but that leopard-headed warrior—he alone has brought this defeat upon us. Wouldn't you agree, Marus?"

Amnelis spoke evenly. She saw the change in mood that had come over her officers, and she had ceased to rage against the elusive Guin, transforming the fury she had felt earlier into a deadly calm. What she needed now was a cool head. Her lips did not tremble, even when she spoke of Guin directly. Her legendary icy calm had returned. She had swallowed her pride, convincing herself of the importance of judging her enemy objectively; the change in her attitude was remarkable. Of course, all who were there knew that this lady of ice was far more severe, and far more potent, than the fiery-tempered general of the previous day.

The lord of Tauride Castle nodded his head and spoke, his words heavy on his lips. "As you say, my lady."

Amnelis slowly surveyed the men who stood before her, her impossibly deep green eyes alighting on each in turn.

"The Sem know little of battle," she said after a long silence, "and less of tactics. They are barbarians, trusting only in their sheer numbers to carry the day. This we Mongauli have seen time and time again, at the misfortunate battle of Stafolos Keep and in every skirmish we have had with the Sem on our patrols through the Marches.

"Time and again, they have behaved like witless beasts—until now. Since we crossed the Kes into Nospherus, the Sem have shown remarkable craftiness—guile, even. They use a bewildering variety of tactics, taking advantage of our unfamiliarity with the terrain to lead us into ambushes and traps, like the monster-trap of the yidoh, employing one force as a decoy to divide us while hitting us on the flank with their main army. Assuming that they did not overnight obtain and read Augustinus's *Soldiery* or Alzandross's *Book of Tactics*, we must assume that the recent successes of the Sem are the sole work of the creature known as Guin."

Her gaze flickered across her officers again, turning her last statement into a question. The captains were quick to agree.

"As you say, my lady."

"It cannot be otherwise."

"Surely, it is all the work of that fiend."

"It was our ignorance of him and his influence that led us to view the Sem so lightly, Lady General."

Amnelis nodded slowly. She smiled a fierce smile.

"Then it seems clear that our true enemy is not the Sem,

but rather the leopard-man that leads their army. And he is a shrewd foe! The skill of their assaults, their swift advances and swifter retreats, all reveal his caliber. He is no mere mercenary, or accidental soldier. I believe that, when we do capture this creature and take off that leopard mask, we will find him to be none other than some famous general."

"Surely, you are correct, my lady."

"Or perhaps," Marus added, "we would find him to be the king of some country, a keep-lord, or a hero known throughout the land. Yes, it is as sure as the sand we stand upon."

"Ahh," Tangard nodded, then blurted, "he could even be Gohran. In the worst possible scenario, of course."

The weathered Count Marus drew his long white eyebrows together, frowning. "Tangard. If you say that in jest, you jest poorly."

"No, no—I meant no jest, Elderlord," Tangard responded. "Rather, I mean to say he could have been sent by Kumn or Yulania. As you can see from the current situation, it is quite possible that one of our archduke allies has joined hands with the enemies of Mongaul to, ah…put us in our place, so to speak." Tangard stroked his ruddy moustache in thought. "And there are many warriors of name in our allies' lands, Gandar the Grappler, Och-Ran of the Blue Whiskers. Could this leopard-man be one of them?"

"What we can say for sure is that he is no Mongauli traitor," Amnelis spoke with the faintest hint of a cold smile in her voice. "For, to my certain knowledge, there is not one warrior in our homeland that could do what this man has done alone."

A barely noticeable shiver passed through the men. It lasted only a moment, but in that moment Count Marus straightened and looked warily at Amnelis. It was clear he did not approve of what the young lady-general had said.

But it seemed that Amnelis did not notice the tension in the air her words had caused. She turned to speak to Gajus, who had been hovering in the shadows behind her.

"Gajus."

"My lady?"

"Tell me. In all your study, all your readings of the tales of the world, have you learned of any warrior, hero, or king that could be the equal of our adversary—that might, indeed, be the face beneath that leopard mask?"

"Ah, yes…a perplexing question, indeed. Who could it be?" muttered Gajus, sinking into thought under the heavy cowl of his black robe. After a time his voice came hollowly from his unseen face.

"To the extent of my knowledge, there are several men of name in the lands we know who possess both the skill with a blade and the ability to command troops that he has demonstrated.

Gandar of Kumn and Yulania's General Och-Ran of the Blue Whiskers, both just mentioned, would qualify, perhaps. In Cheironia to the north, there is Darcius the Thousand-Dragon and Adan, the Thousand-Tiger, both generals of renown. And in Parros, Adlon, Lord of Kravia…

"Also there is the Black Prince Scaal of Earlgos; the intrepid Andanos, wealthy merchant and chancellor of the free city port of Rygorl; ah, and the Count of Taria, Guy Dolfus. Further to the north, there is Owin Longorn of House Longorn, or perhaps Raider-King Sigerd of Taluuan—it is said that he is an accomplished warrior, and sheathed in muscles like some titan out of legend—"

"Who else in Parros?" Amnelis cut in.

"In Parros?" The runecaster hesitated for a moment. "Well, there is the Holy Knight Darkan, pride of the Holy Knights. But he was wounded in the War of the Black Dragon, and I have heard that he has been bed-bound with his injuries ever since. Of course, Mad Duke Bek is strong enough, and I know for a certainty *he* was not wounded, for he was away when the fighting started, in Earlgos visiting Princess Ema, who had only just been sent there to wed the king. How vexing it must have been for him to miss the battle! We also have the Duke of Crystal, Aldo-Narisse. He was the henchman of High King Aldross, and it is rumored that he took a sharp blow to the head in the battle for the crystal city and was taken captive, though he afterwards escaped and now runs fugitive with a great bounty of gold on his head. We don't know where he is, but I hardly think he wears the leopard-mask, for it was widely whispered that the Duke of Crystal was something of a dandy—a fair boy, who liked to recite poetry—from which I surmise he could not be the great warrior we face here now.

"Of course, it could be—"

"No." Amnelis's sharp voice cut through Gajus's droning recitation.

All there straightened and turned to her.

"He is none of these men," said Amnelis. Her voice was harsh, but her eyes were clouded as though she was looking at something impossibly far away. A crease formed in the smooth skin between her brows, and she spoke cautiously, as though to keep any trace of emotion from her voice.

"I brought up the name of Parros because, given that our foe is defending against the armies of Gohra, it seems to make more sense to me that we should look first to Parros to find the identity of this masked creature before casting our thoughts to far-flung Rygorl or Taluuan. Furthermore, though all the names Gajus has spoken here have merit, none are he."

Amnelis looked around the pavilion.

"The leopard-man is no sellsword, nay, he is not even a

knight, nor a general. I knew from the first time I saw him: he is a king. Nothing less. He was surely born to a house of power, a house that gives decrees, leads men, and is followed in turn—a house with none above it but the gods."

All in the pavilion were silent.

"Of course, there is another possibility!" broke in Gajus at last, seeing his opportunity to resume his lecture, and unable to sit still in such complete silence long without saying anything. "This is nothing more than rumor, but according to some..."

Amnelis glared at the caster.

He continued undaunted. "There are those who believe that, during the Black Dragon War and the invasion of Parros, while our armies were most successful in capturing the king and queen and all their royal insignia, that these were nothing more than decoys—fakes! That is to say, that His Holiness Aldross the Third secretly escaped and is still alive today!"

The captains gasped and said nothing.

Amnelis bristled. "You are saying the leopard-headed warrior is the high king of Parros?"

"It is just a theory, my lady, a theory."

"If this *theory* should begin making the rounds of our camp, I will hold you personally responsible, Gajus, and you know the price of my displeasure is high."

"As you say, my lady," squeaked Gajus, cowering in rather exaggerated deference.

"Any other theories to share?"

"The...world is vast," began the caster tentatively, "and true heroes are as rare as stars on a cloudy night. Indeed, upon further consideration, I do not find it likely that Chancellor Andanos of Rygorl would come to the aid of the Sem, and I've heard no rumor that the Black Prince of Earlgos rode to Parros's aid, bound to them by marriage though he was. But there is one last possibility, though even I would find it quite remarkable if this were the case, and I consider myself rather charitable when it comes to believing the outlandish; and that is a rumor that originates among the unique cultures of the Northlands of Norn, from Taluuan at the southern edge of the snowlands up to Queensland and Migard. Among these realms there is a kingdom by the name of Vanheim. It is said that the king who reigns there, the hero Bardor, is a swordsman and a warrior of a level rare in all the history of our world."

"The hero-king Bardor of Vanheim, yes," Amnelis nodded.

"Furthermore, I think that since most men of the southern lands have skin ever darkened by the sun, and that those who live in the eastern kingdoms are marked by the unique olive shade of their skin, we can wisely guess by the copper skin of our leopard-man adversary that he hails from either the Middle

Country or the Northlands. Ahh, but wait!" Gajus put a hand to his mouth.

"Gajus?" prompted Amnelis sternly.

"I've just remembered something. If you sail down the Kes River, down through the length of the Middle Country, where do you arrive at last?"

"The Lentsea, of course."

"Correct, the Lentsea! And if you sail across its depths, then you will eventually come to Corsea where floats the great island of Simhara, where, it is said, the kings for generations have followed the peculiar custom of concealing their true features behind the gem-encrusted mask of a beast! Still, I suppose it would be presumptuous to say that this leopard mask is likely of the same stock..."

"Simhara," muttered Amnelis. "An island country of legend. There is a labyrinth there, no?"

The runecaster nodded.

"Gajus."

"My lady?"

Amnelis's eyes had opened wide, as though something had startled her. "Simhara—the word itself means 'the lion's country,' does it not?"

"Yes...yes it does," the aged caster replied, then looked up at Amnelis, waiting for her next words.

But those words did not come. Amnelis seemed to have sunken into deep thought. Outside the pavilion, the dark had grown deeper, the gloom heavier, pushing down on the fearful soldiers as they went about their preparations for the night ahead. Only one stood still in the gathering dusk—the young captain Astrias—his black eyes fixed on Amnelis, filled with a sad reverence for the Lady of Mongaul.

2

The deep cold night dragged on.

It was the third night since the Mongauli army had marched into the Nospherus interior. In the camp, the men waited eagerly for dawn, swallowing their unease and the faint longings for home that inevitably crept into their hearts whenever the sun sank below the horizon.

There was only a *twist* of the sand clock to go before sunrise. The small campfires spluttered under the black tarpaulins that had been rigged to hide their light from distant enemies. The faint, shrill hissing of the embers provided a staccato treble to the bone-chilling rumbling bass of the desert wolves' howls that came from afar across the sands. The night was the domain of the desert-dwellers. The men huddled close, casting their thoughts ahead to morning.

A knight sat up from his sandy pallet with a scraping of armor that woke the man sleeping next to him. The second man's eyes opened wide.

"What? What is it?"

All of those who were not on duty were trying to sleep. They had to rest, if only a little, to prepare for the coming long march. More than that, they knew the battle that would surely come during the day ahead would exhaust them even further. But the nighttime raids had put their nerves on edge. Desperately though they wished for it, many felt all hope of rest slipping away.

They were filthy and uncomfortable. The army's scouts had yet to find an oasis where they could replenish their crucial water supplies, and so water had been severely rationed; the men were forbidden to wash their faces or hands. Caked with dust and blood, the once-resplendent Mongauli knights looked worn and diminished.

The sitting knight rose to his feet.

"Nothing. Can't sleep. I'm going to walk the bounds." His horse, sleeping at its tether nearby, gave a startled snort and then dozed again.

"Better not," grunted his neighbor. "It's dangerous. Never know where those wildlings are hiding." He sat up. "Want me to come with you?"

"No. No need. I'll be right back."

The wakened knight furrowed his brow. Saying nothing

more, he settled his body, still encumbered in his heavy, uncomfortable armor, back down on his pallet and closed his eyes with a sigh of resignation. Maybe he'd be able to get a little sleep—a little *peace*—if only a *twist*'s worth... But his tongue was rough and dry in his mouth, and his eyes stung with sand. He quietly adjusted the steely helm that served as his pillow and tried to coax the slightest bit of comfort out of his hard bedding. No matter how robust the men of Mongaul were, he thought, two more days of hard marching and they would all look like a child's toy soldiers made out of mud, exhausted and useless for any purpose.

The knight who had risen took off his helmet and let his face feel the cool night air. He ambled slowly between the black huddled shapes of half-asleep horses toward the outskirts of camp. His fellows, lying curled up on the ground as they sought fruitlessly to steal sleep from the relentless night, heard his footfalls crunch in the sand and lifted their heads. Only when they saw that he was neither a foe nor a messenger come to tell them of some attack did their heads sink back down into postures of sleep. Even in the darkness the knight could sense the tension and irritation all around him.

He reflected on how much the army had changed in a scant few days. He could almost hear the soldiers laughing as they had on the many nights before when they sat around the watchfires, talking of their homelands. Those nights, some of the men had even pulled out flutes and played the merry tunes of camp and tavern. But tonight, the Mongauli army was as silent as the night was black.

Skirting around the sleeping men, the knight moved toward the camp perimeter.

"Who goes there?" came the sharp voice of a spear-wielding sentry. The Sem night raids had taught the guards to be suspicious of every sound.

"Name's Eku, Troop Argon, Marus Corps."

"Your business?"

"Just getting some fresh air."

"Don't go too far, sir."

"I won't—I know the rules."

The blue knight frowned. He hated being treated like a child—he was a soldier, experienced enough that he did not need to be reminded of his orders. He yawned and ostentatiously marched off in the opposite direction.

He kept along the outskirts, walking at a leisurely pace. The cool air on his face was refreshing.

"Hey."

A low voice sounded from the shadows. Eku started, then turned to peer in the direction of the voice. "Who's there?"

"It's me. Hey, can ye lend me a hand, here?"

"What?" Eku searched for the speaker, his eyes squinting suspiciously. He was standing near a small rift that ran through a rocky area just outside the camp, even darker than the open desert. He could vaguely make out some indistinct black lumps in the darkness, but it was difficult to tell whether these were men and horses or just more rocks.

He couldn't find the source of the voice. Eku craned his neck, opening his eyes wide to see through the shadows. "Something the matter?" he asked the empty night.

"Yeah. Can ye lend a hand? Me horse here caught his foot in one o' these blasted crags and now he's stuck."

"Ach," cursed Eku, spitting. "He's got a peasant for a rider, no doubt." The voice was coming from the darkest shadows, just between two dim circles of light made by the torches of two sentries far off to either side. Neither sentry was paying Eku any attention, if they could see him at all. "Hey, where are you? How am I supposed to see you in this blackness?"

"Ah, sorry, sorry. I'm over here—look, I'll come get ye."

One of the dark lumps Eku had taken for a boulder suddenly split into two halves, and one of the halves stood up. Eku could now see the shape of a tall man walking towards him.

"Fine place to have a spill—I'm surprised the Sem didn't find you," Eku grumbled. As the man approached, he could see that he, too, wore the armor of a blue knight. Eku relaxed, his initial feelings of suspicion beginning to abate.

The man stooped a bit, looking in Eku's direction, then he bowed slightly in thanks. From under his helm, obsidian-black eyes glinted in the light of the torches. He straightened up and took another step forward. "Who were ye, again?"

"What? I'm Eku, of Troop Argon. You?"

"I'm from Talos Keep. Look, we'd better hurry. Me horse won't stay still-like. Any longer and he'll break a hoof, he will."

"What were you thinking? If your mount breaks a leg in this desert, you'll have nothing to look forward to but a hell-march. Unless you *want* to be a footsoldier, eh?"

"There's naught I can do 'bout it. If me horse is battered up too bad, well, I guess I'll just have to take one o' our fallen comrade's mounts. He won't be like to miss it!" chuckled the man, grabbing Eku by the hand. "Come on, then."

"Eh? Where's this horse of yours?"

"Here, right over here."

"What were you doing this far out of camp? The sentries will have a harsh word with you, for sure."

The man rambled on, "Guess ye could say I'm a loner o' sorts. Don't like being stuck in with the rest o' the men, see? Too crowded. But it's no worry, me troop's used to it by now."

"Where was your horse again?" asked Eku, looking around. "I don't see any horse around here."

"I'll be damned. That's bloody odd. He didn't get loose himself and run off, now, did he?"

"Well I see nothing, not even a sand flea—hey..." Eku squinted suspiciously. An uncomfortable thought had just occurred to him. "You're from Talos, right? What did you say your name was? Wait!" Now Eku stopped. Talos Keep was garrisoned by black knights, not blue, and the black knights' section of the camp was well to the north! Eku was about to question his errant friend when the man called to him with urgency in his voice.

"You, Eku. Quickly! Here, take a look at this!" The man turned away from him and stooped down to pick something up off the ground.

Eku walked over, trying to see what it was. He noted that the man's armor was indeed that of a blue knight, like his own, which made him wonder all the more why he claimed to be from Talos. All of Marus's men were garrisoned at Tauride!

"Listen—" he began, leaning in to see what it was the man held in his hand.

He never finished his question. Something flashed silvery in the blackness, and there was the beginning of a scream, hurriedly cut off by a hand that darted to cover Eku's mouth.

Then, for a while, there was nothing but a quiet so complete it was stifling. Finally there came a soft thud, much like the sound of a heavy sack of stores falling flat upon the sand.

"Hey!"

A suspicious sentry glanced over toward the sound.

"Something the matter over there?"

There was no answer.

The sentry held up his torch and moved nearer, peering into the gloom between the boulders, but seeing neither the glinting of Sem eyes nor some other horrible Nospherus creature come to feed on human life, he soon went back to his post. He was sure that if he dared to investigate much further—if he went to look out upon the gently rolling dunes, extending like waves across the ocean of night beyond the camp's edge—some unknown horror would emerge and drag him off to the sandy depths.

The sentry made the sign of Janos with his hands and muttered a few words in the old runic tongue. Thankfully, nothing did come out of the desert at him, and convincing himself that what he had heard was a trick of the wind, he went back to his watch.

Back in the camp, the blue knight who had been woken by his fellow rising to go for a walk was still unable to fall back into sleep. *That Eku sure is taking his time.* He had spent several long uncomfortable moments wondering whether he should go check and see whether aught was amiss when at last a blue knight appeared, walking slowly back through the huddled men. His hood was drawn fully over his face and his cloak was buttoned against the chill.

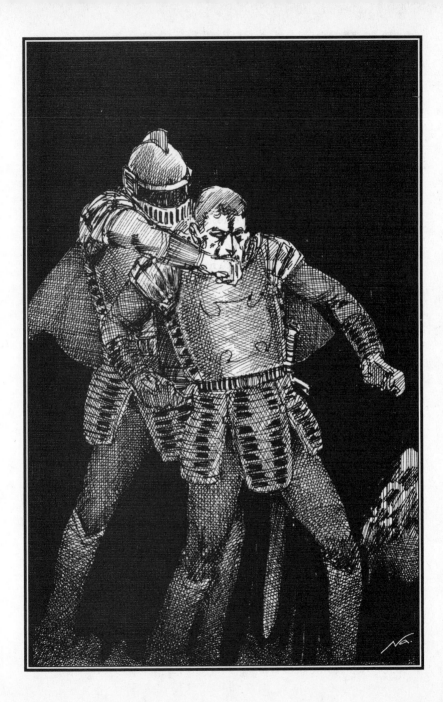

"Eku, that you? Where in Doal's name did you get off to?"

"Ah, didn't go too far," the blue knight grunted back in a voice stuffy with lethargy, as though he had finally attained true sleepiness on his walk and was unwilling to speak too loud and thereby wake himself up again.

"Hmph. You're an odd one, Eku."

The waiting knight's lips were pursed with annoyance. He was on the verge of berating Eku for going off like that and leaving his comrade to worry about what had befallen him, but in the end he just let it go and lowered his head back down.

Dawn would be coming soon. Already, the eastern sky was lightening, as though a thin leaf had been torn from the long book of night. When the morning arrived, they would have another hard march waiting for them, beset on all sides by the wildlings and the creatures of the sand. He would need to conserve his strength. It was not long before he had completely forgotten Eku's strange nighttime stroll.

"Prepare to march."

"Prepare to march!"

Dawn had broken on a night many of the Mongauli thought would never end. The desert mornings, like the nights, came unexpectedly swift and resplendent.

The giant fiery sphere of Ruah lifted above the horizon and

into a harsh blue sky, revealing a landscape softened by no beautiful veil of morning mist, graced by no chirping birds, cheered by no green of dewy grass. Here there were only endless bright waves of sand, linking and shifting and blurring into the distance.

The commander's pavilion was dismantled and packed away and the familiar orders for breaking camp were passed along. Here and there, horses stood waiting for their masters, snorting and scraping the sand with their hooves.

The Mongauli had lived through another Marches night, and their exhilaration at merely being alive spread like a rainbow through their hearts—only to fade, when they remembered that another Marches day was beginning. And day meant that once again in full wakefulness they would have to confront the question of who among them would live, and who among them would have the ill fortune to fall. They did not doubt that this would be another day overwhelmed with cries of war, and billows of burning sand, and the dancing sparks that leap when blade strikes blade, and the sighs of life escaping from dry, swollen lips. Not one among them expected less than painful death.

Already, Death's bleak colors were seeping across the clear Nospherus dawn. The men could sense it. They went about their chores without speaking.

Solemnly the knights gave their horses water and feed, each careful to save one draught for himself, and they chewed their meager breakfasts of jerky and dried fruit. With their supply of water so low, they were unable to prepare their customary morning meal of kneaded-flour gati balls; nor were they permitted to light fires for stewing. The dried meat was so tough that it stuck in their throats no matter how much they chewed. Grimly in the morning light they looked into each other's emaciated faces, then mounted their horses or knocked sand out of their hard boots and tied them on tight for the long march ahead.

"Hey there," the blue knight Evvan of Marus Corps turned nonchalantly to the man next to him, who had already climbed upon his steed. He frowned. "Hey, Eku."

"Eh? Ah?" Eku responded, startled.

"What's wrong? Why aren't you eating? The road is long, don't want you collapsing."

"Don't worry. I'm not hungry right now," replied Eku through the lowered faceplate of his helm.

"Aye, but you should eat all the same. You need to get something in you. 'Can't fight on an empty stomach,' they say. Right?" Evvan quickly tightened his horse's girth, continuing to talk as he checked the fastenings on his saddle. "If you're having trouble getting that jerky down your gullet, I can break you off some of this vasya fruit. My house runs an orchard, you know, and we make it ourselves. It's a might juicier than the bone-parched stuff you get from the company mess."

"Nay, that's fine—I'm fine now. Thanks," replied Eku in the same gruff voice.

Evvan—it was Evvan who had called out to Eku the night before—was a well-meaning sort, if inquisitive. However, he was not the shrewdest of men, nor one who might boast of his soldier's intuition. Thus even as he stood there wondering at his comrade's odd behavior, not once did he draw a connection between it and the strange walk during the night, nor the fact that his companion had kept his faceplate down fully ever since the morning light had broken.

Still, he was curious, and so he asked again, heedless of Eku's attempts to avoid him. "Say, what is it? Not feeling well, are you?"

"Really, it's nothing," the mounted knight replied. "I'll be fine if I stay still a bit. Just leave me alone, will you?"

"Ah, so you are feeling ill! I see. Maybe a touch of the dust-waif fever, eh?"

Eku hastily urged his horse into motion, backing it away as Evvan approached. "Get ready, we're marching!"

"The black knights are riding front today. We've got plenty of time before it's our turn," replied Evvan, now stepping closer and reaching out to get a look under Eku's faceplate.

Just then, a scream shot up from someone—probably one of the sentries—at the edge of camp.

"Wha—" Evvan whirled around to see what the matter was.

As soon as his back was turned, Eku's horse lunged forward, propelling him into the passing stream of riders until he was lost amidst the crowd of knights, rows and rows of men wearing identical blue armor, helms, and cloaks.

Another wordless scream sounded across the sand. The knights stationed near the eastern edge of camp turned in time to see a sentry stumble backwards, his arm pawing the air around him as though he were struggling in some invisible morass. He tried to shout something, but before the words came out, he tripped and fell full length upon his back. The soldiers who were nearest saw a black arrow of familiar design stuck in the very middle of his forehead.

"The enemy!"

"To arms! The Sem have come!"

In a flash, the Mongauli camp was a broiling sea of action.

The knights grabbed their swords and lowered their face-plates, trying to swallow angry sighs of "Not again!" as they fended off the poison arrows that now fell around them like a venomous rain. None had truly believed that the day would pass without incident, but the raids of the night before had been so wearying that they had hoped for at least a brief respite before the new day's battles began.

The way in which the nighttime raiders had struck and then pulled back before the knights could put up a proper defense had clearly been the strategy of one well schooled in the arts of the battlefield. Each attack had come at just the moment when the invaders had decided that there would be no more assaults that night; and then when the knights stood to arms, ready to meet them, the wildlings became scarce as spirits, hidden off in the desert somewhere. It was a tactic intended to exhaust the Mongauli, and it had worked brilliantly.

Marus saw the bleak shadow of fatigue and dismay in the eyes of his men, and he gave a great shout. "Rise, brave warriors of Mongaul! Our enemies are few in number! Crush them now in one blow, and drive these crafty monkeys from the sands forever! Today is the day *we win!*"

"Mongaul!"

The cry went up from all sides as a ripple of excitement passed through the troops. Just then, another voice rose up from the crowd. A knight stood with his arm outstretched.

"The leopard-man!"

All the knights turned in the direction he pointed to see the one whose name was a curse to all the men there.

Whether or not Guin had ever been human, he had now become a god of death in the eyes of the Mongauli. The leopard warrior, mounted on a great charger, was poised alone on the top of a sandy rise high above the Gohran army. His bestial head, silhouetted against the rising sun, streamed like a mane of fire along his mighty neck and gleamed upon the half-bared fangs in his mouth. Huge and hungry, brilliant as the sun itself, he looked down on them with greedy eyes.

"Guin..."

Standing in the heavily guarded center of the camp, Amnelis, the Lady of Mongaul, drew in a sharp breath and muttered a curse against his name. Across the landscape of rushing soldiers, at the head of a line of red knights, the young Astrias saw him, too, and growled between tightly clenched teeth.

"Freak!" Count Marus, his eyes shrouded in wrinkles, but burning no less brightly for his age, swore and spat upon the sand.

All eyes were turned to the strange leopard-headed warrior, as though Guin were the statue of some deity whom the entire Mongauli army had come to worship. Their eyes were filled with hatred, shock, fear, alarm, and burning battle-rage. For that moment, to the more than ten thousand Mongauli who watched him, it was as though their fate had taken form and now shone down on them from the height of that ridge. Whether they wished it or not, they would be led to whatever destiny the beast-man's arms placed before them, like the young boys in the ancient fable who ran off to follow the kitara player to dooms unknown.

The bright, dazzling desert under the white morning sun stretched out to infinity, and the knights and footmen, gazing about, saw themselves in that instant as nothing more than a bleached, ephemeral mirage-army. They were stricken as one with the dread feeling that their destiny might be to chase that sun-drenched, galloping half-man half-beast god until they dissolved into nothingness among the shifting dunes.

It was Marus's hoarse shout that broke the spell and brought them back from their ill-omened hallucination. "What are you doing? He is but one rider! Charge! Take him! *Charge!*"

Even as another rain of arrows fell upon them, a great shout went up as the Mongauli focused their energy and directed their charge towards the rider on the dune.

Quickly the men drew their swords and fell into ranks. It was the beginning of another day of war, blood, and death in Nospherus.

—— 3 ——

It was another bitter conflict in what seemed like an endless string of identical battles for the Mongauli expeditionary army. The sands they fought in, and their foes, never changed.

The tiny Sem, taking advantage of their greatest weapons— their maneuverability and their familiarity with the deadly terrain of their homeland—had so successfully overcome their disadvantage in numbers that they were always on the attack, always pushing back the Mongauli's position.

Perhaps the war-making Mongauli would not have been so dazed were they fighting their fellow Gohrans, or another of the civilized peoples of the Middle Country. At least the folk of Cheironia and Parros, and even Earlgos far to the south, were much the same as them, despite their oft-emphasized regional differences. And while the Steppes had their own culture and the Northlands had another, they had by and large developed in the same direction. But these Sem—no matter how much one looked at them, with their strange chirping cries and their bared teeth—seemed less than men, prehistoric. They were monkeys complete with furry tails. It was hard to believe them capable of possessing any real intelligence.

Even now, there were some among the Mongauli who snorted with indignation at the very idea of drawing swords against "mere primates," and they were hard pressed to summon much of a will to fight.

But an enemy was an enemy, and they were at war. Like great colored swarms that stained the bleached, flat Nospherus sands, fiercely contending masses of some writhing, primordial ooze, the two armies met and skirmished and killed one another.

Far away on the northern horizon, a wall of tall, white mountains stood like a distant mirage. These were the Ashgarns, a range of towering peaks forever capped in ice. On the eastern reaches, the Kanan Mountains of legend stretched away southward in a jagged black line. Far from reminding the Mongauli that Nospherus, too, had its limits, the mountains served only to emphasize the vast, flat desert between them and the horizon, an inhospitable waste that offered no place to hide.

The only noticeable features in this vast sea of sand were the flat area known as the Devil's Anvil, through which the invaders had recently passed, and the rocky hills to the northeast, which, unbeknownst to them, hid the villages of the Sem. It was enough to drive despair into the heart of any man who had grown up surrounded by the rich greenery of the Middle Country. It had an absence of emotion, a feeling of lifelessness, a severity that was utterly inhuman and welcomed nothing that did not belong to the sand.

As they had done two times the night before, the Sem attacked, saw that they had left a mark, and withdrew. But even the flight of the wildlings was disheartening to the Mongauli soldiers, who were eager to beat down and kill every last one of the crafty monkeys and thus put an end to the aggravating and painful raids.

Cries went up from the knights.

"Chase them!"

"They're pulling back! Hunt them down!"

Some stood in their saddles, calling their fellows to the attack, but the messengers of Amnelis, wearing white plumes on their shoulders, were quick to pass the countermand.

"No one is to follow the Sem! Orders! Orders!"

"Assume defensive formation. Prepare to march!"

The aged Count Marus, riding his big charger at the head of the blue knights, looked concerned.

"This will not do," he muttered, lifting his faceplate and furrowing his whitened brows. The only person close enough to catch his words was his lieutenant, Garanth, astride a bay stallion close beside the count.

"I beg your pardon, Lord Captain." Garanth sounded surprised. "Did you say something?"

"No." The count furrowed his brow further.

Garanth eyed the count carefully. "It looks to me that our enemy has been routed, and all is in order in our camp, my lord?"

"I supposed it would seem that way, but it is not. Trust me." Marus spoke softly so that only his lieutenant might hear him. "This turn of events does not sit well with me. Our losses with each raid are slight, and we are quickly growing used to these Sem attacks. We know that each time they appear, they will pull back before long—we've come to expect it like we expect the sun to rise in the morning. That is what troubles me."

"My lord?"

"Garanth, are we not doing exactly as they intend us to do? They attack us when *they* want, and then draw off again when *they* want, while we merely scramble to gather our weapons and fend them off each time. We are responding, always responding—always on the defensive, you see?"

"I see this, my lord, but as you say, our casualties are light, and we still outnumber them. Does that not make the advantage ours?"

"The principles of strategy forbid a policy of mere reaction.

Even a dagger can fell a mighty oak if the oak does nothing. Be they fewer in number, or poorly armed, victory always goes to the side that *acts*, not the side that *reacts*. You would do well to remember this, Garanth: when a battle drags on so, the side that wins is the side that can convince its men that they are attacking and their opponents are defending. It has nothing to do with the advantages of numbers or territory."

Garanth nodded.

"Of course, this is a matter that I should have minded," sighed Marus. He shot a glance towards the gathering of white knights where the army's temporary command post had been established. "Our lady general is young, Garanth—of course, that's not something I would say before our soldiers, either. But she *is* young, and though they call her the Lady of Ice, I can see all too clearly the blush of warm blood beneath her skin. She cannot yet understand these nuances of the battle. That is why she must take better heed of the advice that Gajus and I give."

Garanth nodded, and was silent. Marus smiled at him. "It does little good for me to say these things here, to you. It is just that...I do not like the way things are going."

"Lord Captain, if you are troubled, why not act yourself? You could speak to the lady general again, persuade her to go on the offensive, convince her to hunt down the Sem. I know for a fact that our men are eager to do just this."

"Hmm," Marus grunted and considered the idea for a while. Then his face brightened. "Well spoken, Garanth. I believe that your counsel is good." He favored his lieutenant of many years with a smile. "Perhaps this is the right time, too. The Sem are unlikely to return soon." Marus nodded, then gently nudged his faithful steed's flank and began to move out of formation—but at that very moment he heard Garanth's voice raised behind him.

"What's that? An urgent message?"

He turned to see to whom Garanth was speaking, and saw a tall blue knight with lowered faceplate approaching, bringing his horse to a slow walk and finally stopping next to the lieutenant. The knight nodded vigorously. "Yes, yes, very urgent!"

"Halt!" responded Garanth sharply. "Though this may be an expeditionary force, and we may have left some formalities behind us, have the decency to properly introduce yourself."

"I beg your pardon, sir," replied the blue knight. "I am Eru, of Troop Argon."

"Eru of Troop Argon. Very well, what's your message?"

"Again, I beg your pardon, sir, but if I might speak to the lord captain..."

"The lord count is busy. I will relay the message, you may speak to me."

"Yes, I'm sure, but..." the blue knight floundered.

"What? Is speaking to his lieutenant beneath your station?"

"Garanth, wait." Marus abruptly tugged the reins hard to the right and turned his horse back toward the two men. "Let us hear this message."

The blue knight bowed. "If we might speak where no one else can hear..."

Marus snorted. "We are in formation and in formation we shall stay! Speak quietly, and none but Garanth and I will hear you. I should think that would be sufficient."

"Yes, m'lord," replied the blue knight.

It was the youthful spring in the voice of this Eru of Troop Argon that had brought the count back to hear what he had to say. As a lord in charge of an entire castle, Marus was well practiced in discerning the worth of a man, a fact in which he took no little pride. This Eru's voice was young indeed, almost child-like, yet it possessed a fearlessness and a deep strength that the aged soldier noted with approval.

From behind his faceplate, Eru exchanged stares with Count Marus and Garanth.

It was Garanth who spoke first. "Come on now, show your face. Have you no manners?"

"M'lord," Eru nodded and, somewhat reluctantly, raised his faceplate.

Well now, thought Marus, as something in the man's look struck a chord within him. Then he smiled, realizing what had surprised him about the young Eru's visage. While it was a touch longer, and perhaps a bit harder around the eyes, the knight's face looked much like that of Astrias, captain of the red. Eru's black, canny gaze shone with a lively spirit and met the count's stare straight on without the slightest touch of fear. He was even younger than his voice had led Marus to believe.

"Speak, Eru."

"I... Well, you see, m'lord, I wouldn't want to alarm you with what might amount to supposition on my part—"

"Enough with the preamble. What is it you wish to say?" snapped Garanth irritably.

Eru's eyes flashed back and forth, checking to see that no one else was within earshot. "Well, it's this: I believe I may know whence this leopard-headed creature comes. I may know who he is."

"What?!" Marus's incredulous voice was so loud that several blue knights around them turned to see what had riled him. A dismissive wave from Garanth turned them back around.

Marus waited for the others to go back about their business, then asked, "Can you assure me of the truth of this claim you mean to make?"

"Well, m'lord, I've not had the opportunity to check beneath that mask and see for certain, of course..."

"None of us have. So, how do you know?"

"Yesterday, in the battle, when he appeared on that dune, I saw upon his chest," here Eru raised his hand and slashed a cross in the air, "a scar."

"That he might have had. He was mostly unclothed. So you recognized that scar, did you?"

"I believe I saw its cutting, yes."

"Hold a moment!" Marus's expression was severe. "This revelation might best be made before the Lady herself."

"I-I would prefer not..." stuttered Eru. "That is, as I said before, I'm not entirely certain, and I wouldn't want to cause a stir without good reason, if you see my problem."

"Yes, I see," replied the count. "Tell us what you know, then, from the beginning. I dare say any inkling of who he is would be better than what we have at the moment." The young blue knight had Marus's complete attention now. The count looked around to make sure that no orders to march had been given, then nodded to Eru. "If what you say is true, it would be valuable information, indeed. Come down off your horse, and stand by my stirrup, and tell me every last detail. We should have plenty of time before the army moves again."

"First," said Eru, more calmly now, his black eyes darting between the two men, "might I receive a promise that this stay between m'lord and his lieutenant, at least until we can be sure who hides behind that leopard mask?"

"You speak far above your station, you—" began Garanth, his eyes flashing, but Marus had become quite enamored of this young knight, and he waved a hand for silence.

"It is no matter," the count told his aide. "With all the lily-livered softlings we get these days, I like a little insolence—shows he's got backbone. Now, Eru, tell us your story."

Eru nodded and dismounted from his horse as he had been bidden, walking over to stand beside the count. "I was born in Gallikea," he began, "and in my sixteenth year I came to Torus. I've been a knight of Mongaul ever since." The young man's voice was clear and crisp as he spoke. "Of course, I was no conscript, but a professional soldier. Before I joined the blue, I wielded the sword of Captain Tagg's red knights, and Lord Roman's black knights, and I fought in numerous battles before I was honored to be part of the Marches patrol.

"My story takes place when I was following Captain Tagg. I had been sent to Luane, capital of Kumn, as a member of the ambassador's guard. As soon as the ambassador, a certain marquis, arrived, he was summoned to the water palace of Archduke Tario, and so we in the guard were relieved of duty for a day, and given leave to tour the city.

"As you know, they call Luane the 'City of Water,' and its beauty rivals that of Tais, the 'Beautiful Monarch' of the south. That day we split up into small groups and idled about, or headed out to buy women, drink wine, and gamble as soldiers do. I was with a small group of close friends, and we went to see the sights. We marveled at the many bridges that cross the city's moats, and we were quite engaged in our exploration when we heard strange voices up ahead of us.

"At first we thought it was a brawl of some sort, but then it seemed like the voices were not arguing, but cheering. The source of the excitement was soon revealed to us. We heard one voice rise above the other shouts with a clear cry of 'Gandar! Gandar!' and soon it seemed that everyone in the streets around us was shouting 'Gandar! Long live Gandar!' in unison.

"'I know this one they speak of,' said a longtime friend of mine. 'Gandar of Kumn is one of the greatest gladiators in the three duchies of Gohra, maybe in all the Middle Country. They say he is the king of fighters, that he can lift two horses with his bare hands, and that no fighter in the last fifty years or the next will rise above him. Heh, of course not! No one dares even challenge him any more. I hear he's so bored with lack of competition that he's taken to showing off by dueling wilderbears and giant vipers—and I daresay they wouldn't fight him either, if they knew what they were up against.'

"Then a shrill voice rang out suddenly right among us, giving us a terrible start. 'You think so, do you?' the voice said. 'Then I daresay you're travelers newly arrived here in Luane.'

"Looking down, I saw that the owner of the voice was a short, shifty fellow with an impoverished look to him and a manner that suggested he was a common panderer of women, or a collector for some gambling den. He sneered up at us, licking his lips unpleasantly, and pulled on the sleeves of our chainmail shirts. 'What nonsense is this?' my companion asked. 'Why, word that Gandar is so strong he lacks competition has even reached our country! Yet to hear you speak, it sounds as if you knew of someone—'

"And here my friend was interrupted by a hundred approaching voices shouting 'Gandar! Gandar!' 'Gandar-King!' and 'Lord of the Gladiators!' and we saw, moving slowly through a wild tide of people cheering his name, Gandar himself. He was riding a chariot over the bridge on which we stood. All of us held our breath.

"Gandar stood arrogantly high, one hand in an iron gauntlet at his waist, and the other clenched in a fist across his chest. Not a move did he make to steady himself on the chariot's rail, yet he seemed not to sway or rock with the vehicle's lurching in the least. He was truly a giant of a man. His skin was like dark-glinting steel that armored his entire body, and the hair streamed from his head like a lion's mane. So tall he was that even I, who, as you can see, am not short among men, felt much like a midget who had wandered into the presence of a titan. His face was as threatening as the rumors told, and the old scars that ran across it made him look all the more impressive, like a machine that knew only how to make war.

"'He is amazing,' muttered my companion. 'I would not have the strength to twist his neck even were he sodden and comatose before me! And you mean to tell us that there is someone to challenge this man to a fair fight? I don't believe it.'

"'I didn't say there *was* anybody,' said the pander, baring his teeth in a grin. 'Why, if there was, I'd be the first to place my bets on Gandar and make a small fortune! All I'm saying is, the world's a large place, and I would *believe* it if someone did show up claiming they could best Gandar.'

"No sooner had the little man finished saying this than a deep, terrible bellow rang out from the slowing chariot. It was Gandar. 'You there,' he shouted in a voice that rattled our very bones, 'What was that you said?' It seemed that, as luck would have it, Gandar himself had somehow heard what the squalid little fellow had been telling us, and it had piqued his interest. The pander was frantic.

"'N-Nothing, sir, just, eh...' he stuttered, the color draining from his face. I thought he would fall dead right there in the street. I do not blame him, either, for that evil-looking gladiator now stopped his vehicle directly before us, his mouth open like a rampant lion's.

"'I heard you! You said that a gladiator strong enough to challenge the great Gandar has appeared! You said it!' roared the giant man. He wore iron bands on his legs and arms, and a hide loincloth that hung down from his waist. The bands clanged together as he jumped lightly down to stand, towering over the unfortunate pander. 'So, at last, I have competition! Excellent. Bring him out. I am Gandar, and I would face the one who says he can best me. I must know if he speaks the truth! Who is he? Where are you hiding him? Is it one of you?'

"Suddenly, Gandar noticed us standing by the pander. His eyes burned holes in our chests. We were quick to deny that any of us stood a chance and nary hesitated to firmly relinquish the honor of a duel. 'Then it must be you!' growled Gandar, glaring at the diminutive pander. The little man looked ready to faint.

"'I-I beg of you, sir... Please, it was just an expression, a s-slip of the tongue, Master Gandar!'

"'Hmph. I know when a man is telling the truth, and I believe you know of someone who would challenge me! Now, tell me where he is. The crowds in this city tire of watching me fight mere bears and snakes. Tell me!'

"The pander cowered in silence.

"'Not talking? Fine. Men! Bring this one to my lodgings!'

"'Help!' squawked the pander, and he spun around and

made to escape, but the gladiator reached out a thick arm and grabbed him by the neck before he could run. He was like a kitten held helpless in its mother's jaws. I believe all of us felt a fluttering in our breasts then. None there had the nerve to stop a man like Gandar, however, and so we stood by and watched him swing the hapless pander back toward his chariot.

"Just then, a deep voice sounded from behind us—from the door to the inn at the foot of the bridge we stood on. 'It does not do to act so childishly, be you Gandar or any other grown man,' the voice said.

"A moment later the speaker stepped out of the inn and stood before the astonished crowd. He too was a giant—easily the equal of Gandar in size—and the long dust-covered mantle and well-worn boots that he wore made us think that he must be a traveler from distant lands. The muscles that armored his massive frame were marvelous beyond compare. Yet it was not his phenomenal size that brought gasps and some cries from the crowd. No, it was the strange black cloth he wore around his head—for when he first appeared in the shade of the inn, the cloth made it seem as if he had nothing from the neck up—as if he were a headless champion come from beyond the grave.

"But, as we looked more closely, it became apparent that he merely wore a bulky wrapping of some sort, with small holes cut for the eyes. Those eyes! They shone with a yellow fire, and just one look at the fearful strength in them was enough to convince us that this, here, was the man of whom the pander had spoken.

"It was not long before Gandar, too, came to this conclusion. He let go of the pander, and gazed at the newcomer, sizing him up. Then a look of joy came to his face, like a desert in bloom after a long-awaited shower. 'Ha, a strong one!' Gandar practically howled in delight. 'You look strong! Fight me, then! I beg you, fight me!'

"'I am not a gladiator,' the man replied.

"'Who cares? I must fight someone strong! Fight me! Here! Draw your sword!'

"'Street fighting is a serious offense.'

"'Then, to the arena! Come!'

"'I will not.'

"It was hard to tell whether the man feared Gandar at all. He seemed hardly even to be engaged in their exchange. The big gladiator could sense this, and he grew more insistent as he challenged the stranger again. When this failed, he became incensed, and drew the short sword at his side. 'Then I will make you fight!' he shouted, and lashed out with his blade, first a cut and then a backstroke, faster than the eye could follow.

"By the time the crowd reacted with a shout, he had slashed the strings of the man's mantle. But that was not all. Beneath the fastenings of his cape, the blade had struck the flesh of the stranger's broad chest, and cut a perfect 'x' across it, sending up blood in a crimson spray.

"What surprised us most about this was not the brazen lawlessness of Gandar's attack, but rather the boldness of the masked stranger who, it seemed clear to us, could have easily avoided his sword, yet instead had chosen—*chosen*—to take the cut without moving so much as a hair.

"Gandar saw this as well as we did, and his face went white as fine paper. Then, in a blur of motion, the man grabbed hold of the gladiator's arm with a hand that seemed to hold the strength of an entire army, and he drew him close. 'I said no,' the man growled. 'I'm not going to fight you now. One day, I would like to fight a man such as you, very much. But now, I have something more important that I must do.'

"'Well, you don't seem like the type to run,' muttered Gandar, his words flat and lifeless, as though he had the wind knocked out of him.

"'If that is your worry, let me tell you my name,' replied the stranger. 'I am...' he began, but the only one to hear the rest of what he said was Gandar himself, for he leaned in close and whispered it in the gladiator's ear.

"Gandar's face went paler than before—and it seemed to us that he shook with fear! 'What?' he muttered, stricken into a daze as he stood there in the street. Before we knew it, the stranger, making no attempt to staunch the blood that flowed freely from the wound on his chest, had disappeared back into the inn.

"We were left only with an unquenchable curiosity, and a lingering amazement at what we had witnessed there that day," Eru concluded, finishing his story.

Count Marus sighed and scratched the beard on his chin and was quiet for a long while. "As you say," he began at last, breaking the thoughtful silence, "this tale gives us no solid proof of our enemy's true identity, but if that man truly was that leopard-headed warrior, then this is no trivial piece of information, Garanth." The count turned to his right-hand man. "Until now, we had feared only that he had allied himself with Parros and the Sem, bringing together the enemies of Mongaul against us. But, if by some chance, he was this hooded man who appeared in Kumn..."

"I, too, was suspicious of the man," offered Eru, "so I went to the inn—it was only later that I found out the pander was an employee of that very same establishment—and tried to dig up some information. But the big warrior had already left for parts unknown and he had left no name in the inn register by which to identify him."

"Hrm," Marus snorted, then looked at the warrior Eru from Troop Argon and considered him. "Very well. I will keep this story to myself. That, and—Knight Eru, you seem to be a man with his wits about him, and an eye for detail—and your sword arm looks strong. You don't belong in one of the regular troops. Come and join my guard. You may be of some use to me."

"It would be an honor, m'lord," Eru declared, drawing the hilt of his sword to his chest in a salute.

"You agree? Good, then bring your horse and fall in with the ranks behind me. I'll inform your troop captain." It was clear from the way the count spoke that this bright youth had made quite an impression on him. "I had no idea there were men of such promise in that troop, Garanth."

"Yes, my lord."

"Did you notice, Garanth, how much he resembles the younger Astrias?"

"I was thinking," the lieutenant replied, "that he also looked much like your son, the Viscount Maltius of Torus..."

"That he does," replied the aged count, thinking of his faraway son as he watched Eru leave. "That he does. He's a soldier of some worth. I think I was wise to recruit him," he added in an undertone, nodding to himself. "Garanth. Please inform Troop Argon of the transfer."

"As you wish, my lord."

"We will be marching soon, I think. Ah, the messengers come even now." Both the count and his aged lieutenant seemed to have completely forgotten about relaying their earlier concerns about the Sem's tactics to the Lady Amnelis.

"March! March!" came the messenger's voice.

Through the commotion and noise of the army's preparations, the loyal Garanth rode back to where the members of Troop Argon were saddling their mounts. He wanted to relay his message before it slipped his mind. "Where's your captain?" he asked one of the men.

"He's busy directing our preparations to march, sir."

"I see," said Garanth, thinking. The sounds of horses whinnying and the clatter of swords and armor around him were deafening. "Then, give your captain a message for me," he shouted over the clamor. "Tell him that Eru of his troop has been transferred to Count Marus's guard."

"Understood," replied the knight, bowing his head.

It was Evvan; and he paused for a moment in puzzlement. *Eru?* he thought to himself. *There's no Eru in our troop that I know of. He must have meant Eku. Yes, come to think of it, I don't see that chap anywhere.*

"Line up!" came a shout from behind him. Evvan jumped, startled, then hurriedly mounted and led his horse into position. Then, like a many-colored beetle crawling out into the sunlight, the Mongauli expeditionary force began to sway and pitch across the white sands of Nospherus. The army was underway again.

— 4 —

"Riyaad...Riyaad!"

The wildling Siba called to Guin several times before the leopard-headed warrior took notice. "Siba? What is it?"

The combined army of the Sem had come to one of the few oases in Nospherus, this one several leagues from the Devil's Anvil. They were camped now on the shore of the broad pool of open water at its center.

"Were you thinking of something, Riyaad?"

The reverie faded from Guin's bright eyes, and he turned to look at the diminutive warrior.

"Garu's men who took the children and elderly to the north have returned," the Sem added.

"I see."

"Riyaad..." A trace of concern had crept into Siba's voice. His furry face, looking as much like a monkey's as a man's, wore an expression of unease that somehow made him seem all the more like a beast. "Is something wrong, Riyaad?"

"I am sorry, Siba. It is nothing."

Guin stood up and stretched to his full height, gazing out over the oasis. It was a strangely quiet, almost peaceful, scene. Improbably peaceful—for here was an entire race caught in a last, tragically desperate fight to survive against an enemy many times greater in numbers.

The oasis was a rare, dramatic accent on the landscape of Nospherus. It lay tucked in a gentle depression in the desert, which was otherwise featureless and flat for miles in all directions save for a few meager rocky hills scattered to the north and east. No trees of any great height grew here, but low shrubs and moss were plentiful. They sucked up the moisture from the air around the pool and grew thick at its edges. It was beautiful, an other-worldly mirage, a cool refuge from the glaring sheets of white sand through which the wildling army had been moving.

Nearly five thousand Sem were newly gathered in this mirage-land, clumped loosely into tribal divisions. They clustered by the water's edge, sipping straight from the pool and stuffing their cheeks with the rich and succulent moss. Once they had quenched their thirst and hunger, they turned their attentions to tending the wounded and fixing broken arrows, mending stone axes, and re-applying poison to their weapons. All were completely engrossed in preparing for the next battle that was sure to come.

"Morale remains high," remarked Guin.

"Of course, Riyaad," Siba replied proudly. "The Sem are a race born to fight. No matter what tribe, no matter man or woman, there is none among us who will cease our struggle. Not until we fall dead in battle."

"That can be a curse as well as a blessing," Guin observed, too softly for Siba to hear him.

"Nospherus is our Mother," the little Sem added. He looked over at his fellow Sem milling about among the shrubs at the edge of the oasis as though they had known no other home from the day they were born. "As long as we are in Nospherus, no matter where we go, or what we leave behind, the Sem are not sad. This, all this, is our land. It doesn't belong to the *oh-mu*. The Mongauli *oh-mu* cannot survive here."

"The humans know this too, but still they come. Siba, humans may fear death, and they may long for their homeland, but sometimes they are driven by something stronger than any of those things."

"This I cannot understand," said Siba, shaking his furry head. He looked up to see Rinda approaching, followed closely by Suni. In her hands the princess carried a simple earthenware bowl. She seemed happy that Guin had returned.

"Guin! I brought your supper. I mashed and stewed it myself!" Rinda held the steaming bowl out with no little pride.

The leopard-man thanked her gruffly and took the bowl, using his fingers to scoop the gruel into his mouth.

"Guin, tell me, when do you next leave camp?" Rinda shot a furtive glance over his muscular body as she spoke, looking to see if any new scars had left their tracks there. Guin grunted, too occupied with his food to answer. Rinda rested her hand lightly on the warrior's elbow. "Guin! I'm part of this army, too, you know. While you're out there fighting, I've been with the Tubai and Rasa women, and they've taught me how to boil the poison and make arrows, and how to tell the herbs and mosses that mend wounds. But I want to go with you! If they'd just make me a bow the right size, I could go out with you and fight the Mongauli!"

"The battlefield is no place for children."

"Now you're sounding like Istavan!" Rinda pouted.

"Where's the prince?"

"Remus is with Loto and the others. He's learning the Sem tongue much faster than me, I'm afraid, and he's having a grand old time." Rinda sighed, but she seemed to have completely forgotten her request of moments before. "Speaking of Istavan, Guin, where has he run off to? You've gone on raid after raid, and he still hasn't returned!"

"Ah, you're worried about him," Guin chided. "He angers you when he's here, but as soon as he's gone, you're lonely?"

"Well, I-I never! He can go get swallowed by a sand worm for all I care!" Rinda's cheeks turned beet red; her head drooped.

"I'll bring some wine," she said, and walked off without even so much as a backward glance. Suni tottered along behind her. Watching her leave, the faintest shade of worry seemed to come over Guin's leopard features.

He is late. Too late. What could he be doing?

Guin's yellow eyes flared. Siba looked up, sensing something. Of course, the wildling had no way of knowing what went on in that leopard head, but of all the Sem, the young Raku warrior had spent the most time with Guin, and he had an inkling of the weight that rested on those broad shoulders. "Riyaad," Siba began—but Guin's thoughts were elsewhere. A low growl spilled from his mouth and he set down his bowl.

"Siba, where are Loto and Ilateli?" the leopard-man asked. His voice was calm, betraying none of his concerns.

"I will fetch them, Riyaad!" Siba exclaimed, springing up to summon the chieftains, but Guin stopped him.

"No, I will go to them," he said, walking briskly down toward the oasis pool.

Cries of "Riyaad! Riyaad!" went up from the Sem as he walked among them, and all stopped their preparations to look up at him. Their eyes shone with a childlike, unsullied trust and a faith in Guin that was complete.

Loto, high chieftain of the Raku, Ilateli of the Guro, Tubai of
the Tubai and Kalto of the Rasa were gathered on the spread skin
of a desert wolf in the shade of a bush, engaged in vigorous debate,
but they stopped and stood as soon as they saw Guin approaching.

"Riyaad," spoke the white-furred Loto in a solemn tone,
"thanks to you, we Sem have won victory upon victory." While
most Sem voices were high-pitched and sharp to the ear, Loto,
who was Suni's grandfather, had a voice that was gravelly and
surprisingly deep for one so small.

"But, Riyaad," said Ilateli of the Guro, "these orders that
you give, to withdraw each time so soon after we taste battle, they
leave me hungry. If we only kept fighting we could drive the *oh-
mu* demons off our sands for ever!"

It seemed that the chieftains had been debating the merits
of Guin's strategy of repeated surprise attacks and retreats and
that they were not all of one mind on the matter.

Ilateli had been wounded in the fighting before, but seemed
to pay his cuts no mind. To the contrary, he seemed the liveli-
est of the bunch, and the fur on the stump that was his tail—the
result of an old battle—bristled with excitement. He was large
for a Sem, standing nearly as tall as Rinda and Remus.

"Ilateli, you are looking at the sand beneath your feet without pausing to consider the horizon. It is because of Riyaad's
leadership that we have come so far," spoke up Kalto of the Rasa.

His strong words came out rather meekly; his tribe was the smallest among those gathered there, and he knew it.

"But we must not forget the Tubai's use of the yidoh. Without the victory of the yidoh, we would have lost long ago!" shouted Tubai of the Tubai.

"This is no time to argue amongst ourselves," said Loto sharply.

"You are right," Ilateli replied. "But I must be allowed to say this one thing. What do we fight for if not to destroy our enemy? With these little raids and retreats we are like a mouth-of-the-desert that sticks the tip of one tentacle out of its sandy lair only to draw it back in again. We will never grab our prey, never drink of its sweet juices!"

"You are wrong, Ilateli," began Loto, but Guin interrupted him:

"No, he is right. It is as Ilateli says!" the leopard-man's booming voice rang out, drawing yelps of surprise from the Sem.

"Riyaad!" Even Siba looked at him amazed.

"Listen to me. I have thought much about what will come next. This strategy I have taught you is meant to chip away at the enemy, but if we go on like this much longer…"

All the Sem chieftains waited in silence for his next words.

"If we go on like this for even three more days, the Sem will surely lose."

Kalto screeched in disbelief. Loto and Ilateli's eyes stabbed at Guin. Their ears perked forward, not wanting to miss a single word.

From behind them, Rinda came carrying a jug of wine, followed closely by Remus and Suni. Sensing the tension on the air, the princess set down the jug and took her brother's hand. Silently they stood, staring at the leopard-headed warrior.

"You say the Sem will lose. Why, Riyaad?" Siba demanded. His shrill voice broke through the veil of silence that had settled upon the chieftains. "You were the one who told us that we should fight this way—your way. We are hurting the army of the *oh-mu*, you said. The *oh-mu* are only a few times our number. If we keep hitting them, soon, they will have no more than us!"

"Yes, Siba, we are hurting them—but we are losing our own too," Guin replied curtly. "I've thought about what we must do, and I've done all I could to ensure we will have a chance of dealing a death blow to our enemies. But even if all goes perfectly, the Sem army lacks a trump card!"

For a moment there was quiet. Then Siba spoke up worriedly. "What is a trump card, Riyaad?" While the Sem language was amenable to simple logic and concepts such as honor, it was not well suited to abstraction, and certain human idioms did not translate well.

"I mean that, if we continue merely to throw dust in our

enemies' eyes as we have been doing, we will lose what advantage we have within three or four days at the most," Guin explained. "We have been on the offensive till now, and our enemies are on unfamiliar territory. They are confused, and their spirit is beaten. However, if we keep fighting them in the same way, we will become predictable, and they will be able to adapt. They will seize on the facts that their losses are light and that the Sem army is still fewer in number, and they will realize that our feints are meant to conceal this from them. Then we are finished. They will go on the offensive, down to the last man, and we do not have the strength to repel a full frontal attack by ten thousand elite soldiers. If we had that kind of power, we would have already crushed them in the raid this morning."

The Sem chieftains exchanged looks.

"But, Riyaad," Siba pleaded, "I do not understand all that you say. Before, when we gathered in the village of the Raku, you told us that if we did what you told us to do, if we followed your strategy, we would win! You told us that Nospherus was our ally!"

"Yes, and it is because we have Nospherus on our side that the battle has gone favorably for us, so far," Guin replied. "But the yidoh were a one-shot trick, and the enemy is no longer surprised by our surprise raids. Ideally, the timing is right for us to attack with our hidden main force—to deal a crushing blow. But we have no main force. That is the trump card, the secret weapon, that we lack. If the conflict continues as it has, then even if the plans I have laid pay off temporarily—no, especially if they pay off—the Sem will lose."

"What of the secret plan for which Istavan now prepares the way?" Loto demanded. "When you told us of that, you said it could save us!"

"It could, for a time. It could deal a terrible blow. But we need no less than complete victory, and we have nothing yet that could give us that."

"So we will lose?" screeched Ilateli, slamming a fist on the sand.

Guin's feline eyes turned and met the wildling's. His gaze was imperious.

"No! To lose would mean death. And that is not an option. What I have been considering is how big a gamble we must make in order to give ourselves a chance of victory."

"A gamble?" asked Loto.

But at that moment a young Sem of the Raku came running into the midst of their gathering. "Riyaad!"

The youth, a scout, clutched a rolled sheet of coarse reed-paper in his hand. "Riyaad! We did as you said, and went out when the *oh-mu* marched again, and in their abandoned camp we found this under a cactus!"

"You found it!" shouted Guin, snatching the paper from

his hand. He read it intently, and a fire kindled in his eyes. "Excellent!" he growled, and tossed the sheet aside. Then he slapped his knees and stood. "Chieftains of the Sem, preparations have been made. Keep to yourselves all that I have said here."

"Of course, Riyaad," Ilateli replied stiffly.

Rinda and Remus exchanged curious glances. Then as one they bent down and snatched up the discarded paper. Spreading it flat, they saw that it was marked with a string of mysterious words written in crude hen scratch letters:

"Preparations / finished / await signal / smoke"

Below the letters was a half-legible mark that looked something like two snakes intertwined.

"Guin..." began Rinda, thinking to ask him what it meant. But her words failed in her mouth as she looked at the leopard warrior.

He stood near her, one hand at his waist, his body still as the carven sculpture of a giant. And suddenly it seemed as if his mighty figure emitted a white blaze of fire, so bright it was hard to look at. For a moment Rinda was gripped by the irrational fear that if she touched him she would be burned.

Guin...

It was as though she could see his superhuman will, his decisive power, with her naked eyes, and the sight of it drove from her mind all thought of questioning him about his plans or purposes.

"Ilateli! Loto! Siba!" barked Guin. "You remember the preparations. You can carry them out, even if I am gone?"

"Of course," Ilateli shot back.

"But, why, Riyaad?" ventured Siba.

"Listen to me, Sem warriors," shouted Guin, sweeping his powerful gaze over all the tribesmen gathered around them in the oasis. "We are winning for the moment, but if we continue to fight as we have done, we will surely lose. Yet there is another path we might follow, one that will allow us to avoid this loss— and more. We can seize victory and drive the *oh-mu* from Nospherus forever!

"Do you have faith in me? If you have faith, then you will need to hold out for a full four days, and four alone. Listen..."

Guin began to tell of his plan. Before long the cries of the Sem rose around him in waves, full of amazement and surprise, but the mighty warrior's voice only boomed the louder as he spoke on, explaining how they would defeat the army of Mongaul.

Chapter Two

THE DEPTHS OF THE DESERT

I

The white, rolling sands stretched toward the horizon in every direction. The waste seemed endless, a wilderness as vast and featureless as the ocean, until a small shape appeared—a yellow-white blur looking much like a mirage in the distance. It was like a dollop of cream that had been scooped from some hidden saucer and laid upon the sand. But slowly the creamy blur began to sway and grow, and as it grew, it grew more threatening, taking on the form of a towering cloud that prowled like a hulking creature across the cowering land, its tail growing long behind it.

"Not good," muttered the traveler under his breath. He had been watching the thing unblinking for a short while, and now he raised his hand before his eyes as if to shield himself from the reality of what he was seeing. "A sandstorm. I only hope it will change course, or else..."

He shook his head—a head that was not human, but covered

in spotted fur, split by a broad maw full of sharp bright teeth, and set with two tufted ears that lay flat against the fur. The traveler was Guin, the leopard warrior, and he was not pleased.

The trackless waste before him was scored by thousands of rifts and rises in the sand. He clutched the reins of his horse. Over his customary loincloth he had worn a thick leather cloak, and in his saddlebags were packed a quantity of foodstuffs and several skins of water, sufficient stores for a long journey. He had brushed off the concerns and accusations of the Sem and spurned the wishes of Rinda, Remus and the young warrior Siba to join him and had galloped off alone into the depths of inner Nospherus.

His leave-taking had not been easy.

"The Sem will lose. If we sit here, all we have to look forward to is eventual defeat and slaughter at the hands of the Mongauli. But, I have a plan," he had announced with confidence. Yet when he revealed his designs to the gathered Sem, shouts of disbelief, suspicion, and even anger rang through the camp.

"The Lagon? He cannot be serious!"

"Alphetto! The Lagon?"

"Has Riyaad gone mad?"

All the warriors in the camp came to see what the commotion was, and as the word of what Guin had said passed from mouth to mouth, more shrieks of shock and worry rose from the crowd.

"Guin, Guin! What's going on?"

"Guin!"

Rinda and Remus ran up to the leopard-man and tugged at his arms. They still did not know enough of the Sem tongue to understand what he had said, but the reaction of the Sem made the import of his announcement clear.

"Please, Guin, tell us! What did you say to scare them so? We have a right to know too!" Rinda squeezed Guin's massive hand tightly with her own slender one and stared into his emotionless yellow eyes.

"I told them something they should have already realized. If we continue our current strategy, the Sem position will soon be compromised, and we will lose. That is why I must go to gather reinforcements. I've told them to wait for my return."

"Reinforcements?" Remus exclaimed. "Where will you find those?"

"Ah!" Rinda put her hand to her mouth to stifle a shocked cry. Suddenly, she understood what it was that the Sem had been clamoring about. "Guin! You don't truly mean to go to—to *them*, do you? The Lagon? You would make allies of the Lagon to fight against the Mongauli?"

"Precisely."

Of all the bizarre plants and creatures—and things in-between, like the yidoh—that chose the terror-filled wilds of Nospherus as their home, only two bore any resemblance to humankind: the diminutive Sem and the mysterious Lagon. To the civilized peoples of the Middle Country, the Lagon were even more fearsome than the primitive, monkey-like Sem. It was said they were as giant as the Sem were small, standing far taller than most men, and that they were wild and violent, a fierce, sub-human race. Yet in truth there were few human folk even in the oldest stories who had ever met with the elusive creatures; little indeed was known about the giants of Nospherus.

The Sem at least were familiar to the Gohrans and other homesteaders who dwelt near the Kes. Certain of the Sem tribes frequently left their villages in the hilly area in the northeast of Nospherus and crossed the black river, skirmishing with the Marches patrol and raiding the villages on the western banks. Nor was it uncommon for the Marches patrol to foray briefly across the Kes on punitive expeditions.

The Lagon, by comparison, were an enigma, a legendary race shrouded in mystery. They lived deep in the Nospherus interior. According to one story, they could be found far across the desert, shielded by mountains where they hewed their homes straight from the solid rock. Another legend held that they were the true nomads of Nospherus, desert drifters that moved from one place to the next, possessing neither homes nor material wealth of any substance, spending their days wandering the endless Nospherus sands.

Or perhaps neither of these tales was true. After all, other than Cal Moru, the magus of Kitai, no known person from civilized lands had ever crossed the demon wastes and come back alive, so there was no way of confirming anything about the lands beyond the Kes. To the people of the Middle Country, all of the lands around that black river were simply known as "the Marches"—a treacherous borderland, full of terrors best avoided. And even to the wildling Sem, who had lived for ages in the very midst of the Marches wastes, the Lagon were little more than a myth.

So it seemed to those at the oasis camp that when Guin left them, carrying the fate of the desert wildlings in his hands, he went in search of a fearful legend. Loto and the other Sem chieftains had resisted, of course; even if some among them had not suspected him of using the dubious plan as a pretext to escape from certain death at the hands of the Mongauli, it nonetheless worried them all to lose their leader, the very one who had brought them every victory they had won against the invaders so far. All of Guin's power of persuasion and persistence had been necessary before their objections were overcome at last. But there was one against whom no amount of persuasion worked. It was

Rinda, more than any other, whom Guin had to work mightily to convince.

"I don't care what happens, Guin. All I know is that I will not be separated from you again! Whether you go to the Lagon, or to Doal's very doorstep, it makes no difference to me. I am going with you—and so is Remus! You *will* take us with you, Guin!"

It took even the leopard-headed warrior some time to work up the courage to answer Rinda's adamantine decree. "You speak the impossible. This is no sightseeing trek."

"I assure you, idle travel is the furthest thing from my mind!" Rinda replied hotly.

"Time is of the essence," Guin explained, "and the desert is filled with unknown dangers. Don't you realize what a hindrance you two would be?"

"Perhaps, but if we were there, we could go for help should you need it! And, if we were with you, we wouldn't have to sit here wondering whether you had failed, or succeeded, or were in some sort of fix..."

"Little princess," Guin said softly, moved by Rinda's earnestness. "Trust in me, and wait. I will not fail."

"I-I know you won't fail, Guin. But, you might need help, another pair of arms or legs—or someone like me, someone with the spirit-sense, Guin. And then it would be too late."

"Little princess, there is no time. Every *twist* wasted brings us closer to peril. I'm leaving at once."

"But Suni says you've not packed yet!" said Rinda tearfully. Remus looked at her, his eyes filled with worry. He, too, found it hard to be separated from the leopard-man, but he thought first of Guin's wishes, and he realized the futility of trying to accompany him through the many difficulties and dangers that surely lay along his path. He was too realistic to recklessly give in to his heart as his sister did.

"Rinda," he said softly, touching her hand.

"I don't care, I'm going where you go, Guin, and no one can stop me. I've made my decision!"

Guin looked long at the little girl, her chin thrust out forcefully and her gaze unwavering, and he chuckled and shook his golden head.

"I will tell you why you must stay—both you and your brother, Prince Remus. If you do not, the Sem will not condone my plan. They will think only that I have taken you away to safety before things fall apart, and that I have abandoned them to die."

"So, we are to be hostages," said Remus evenly.

"Yes. That, or the chieftains, Ilateli in particular, will not trust me. Unlike Loto, he has not given me his unconditional loyalty, and I do not expect it from him."

"Then why not just leave Remus and..." Rinda began, but

her voice failed her and she snapped her mouth shut. She felt suddenly that she had herself caught in a painful dilemma. A powerful impulse from deep inside made her want to follow Guin; yet she was tormented by the thought of parting with her twin brother. In all their life, only once had she been separated from him for more than a few hours, and it was not an experience she cared to repeat. She bit her lip and was silent.

The word came from a tribesman of the Raku that the preparations for Guin's departure had been made. Guin laid his hands on the twins' silvery heads. Rinda seemed about to cry, and Remus stared at him with anxious eyes.

"Listen," he said. "I will find the Lagon, persuade them to join our cause, and return to the battlefield by sundown four days hence. That is my warrior's promise to you." Rinda opened her eyes wide and looked up at the strange warrior-creature who had become her guardian. "In fact, I may come back sooner," he rumbled. "In any case, I must do this. Don't forget I've promised to take both of you to Earlgos or Parros or some other safe haven in the Middle Country. That means that, first, I have to lead the Sem and break the Mongauli army. Trust in me, and wait here." Guin nodded, then with greater force he repeated, "Trust in me."

Rinda made no reply. Her eyes were always quick to show emotion and now they belied the indignant set of her lip, sending large tears rolling down her face.

"Guin, come back soon!" Remus pleaded, reluctantly releasing the leopard-man's arm.

Guin nodded again, then turned and walked with long strides toward where the Raku warriors waited. They were gathered around a horse—a tall muscular stallion with a shiny coat, the healthiest of the many steeds they had captured from the Mongauli on their raids. The charger Guin had ridden previously was now weary from repeated battles, and he had decided to retire it.

"Riyaad! Here is your new mount. Shall we provide you with another, a spare?"

"No need," Guin replied. "Horses are not made for traveling far in Nospherus in any case." He checked the fit of the saddle and donned his thick leather cloak.

"There is alika juice—yidohbane—in the satchel in front of your saddle. And here is an ointment you may put on your arms and legs, any place where skin is exposed; it will keep off the sand leeches and vampire flies."

Guin scooped up some of the thick, moldy-smelling muck the Raku held out to him. It seemed to have been made by mashing up various types of oasis moss. Siba and several other Raku youths helped him apply the runny paste until all his skin was stained a mottled green.

"We've put four days' worth of food in your saddlebag."

Guin nodded.

"Riyaad." Siba paused, his hands still clutching two clots of the green moss-paste, and looked up at Guin. The loyalty he felt for the leopard-headed warrior burned in his eyes. "Siba will go with you."

"No, Siba," said Guin. "I am racing against time, and I will go most swiftly by myself. Besides, I need you to help carry out the strategy I described to you last night. I can count on you to help smooth the differences among the chiefs."

Siba nodded. He could see from the set of Guin's eyes that his decision was final. "Then hurry back, Riyaad," he said in a weak voice. "I fear our spirit will die if you do not return soon."

"I will be back, leading powerful reinforcements behind me, by sundown on the fourth day. This I promise."

"And if you do not return," Ilateli approached Guin as he made to mount his horse, "then we will know that you have abandoned us, and we will sacrifice the two *oh-mu* children to Alphetto, as is the way of the Guro."

"Ilateli!" said Loto sharply.

Guin nodded and lightly leapt astride his horse. "Loto, Siba, Ilateli, everyone, you must battle on as you have done for four more days. Use the strategy we have discussed, and try to hold out against the Mongauli." Mounted, Guin towered gigantically above the Sem. His leather cloak rustled in the wind. "I will return with the Lagon. I promise this." He gave his horse a swift kick in the side and at once it broke into a canter.

"Riyaad!" shouted Siba, and the cry went up from every group of warriors gathered there in the oasis.

"Riyaad! Riyaad!"

"Aii aaai!"

The Sem on all sides gave a great war cry, but there was a tinge of sadness in their voices. Some of their fierce spirit had gone out of them. Their hero, their god of victory, was leaving.

"Hyah!" Guin urged his horse out of the oasis hollow. He planned to head north to search for traces of the Lagon.

"Guin! Guin!"

A shrill voice sounded behind him. Rinda was running in his horse's sandy wake, yelling desperately.

"Guin, east! Go east! Over the Dog's Head. The Lagon are beyond the white rock, where the white stones dance upon the black mountain! Guin! There you will find the soul of the Lagon! Beware the death-wind!"

The princess kept yelling, but Guin was moving quickly and he could make out no more of her words.

The leopard-man raised his right hand and waved with his curled horsewhip to signal that he had heard the girl's directions. He knew that Rinda's words came straight from the gods themselves; she had communed with them, used her farsight, and prayed to Janos so that none of Guin's precious time be wasted. Not for one moment did he doubt the truth of what she said. He swung his mount's head to the right and headed due east, cracking his whip till he was at a full gallop.

The horse made good time, its hooves sending up white clouds of sand until the oasis, and the Sem, were far behind. The cries of "Riyaad! Riyaad!" and the trickling of water were lost in the howl of the wind. Guin was alone in the desert.

Already a half-day had passed since his departure. For a time, he had galloped through changeless scenery over flat, hard ground. Near the oasis, gray lichens had graced the boulders and here and there, desert lizards could be seen darting from one rock-shadow to the next. But as he went farther even the occasional plant became a rare sight, until at last he and his steed were alone, the sole living shapes amidst the winding and shifting featureless sand.

Guin was heavy but he was a skillful rider, and his horse moved swiftly and lightly through the dunes. The Raku had fixed thick leather booties over each of his mount's hooves to help prevent them from slipping and sinking in the sand. The padded hoof-falls sent up a *puff-puff-puff* of sandy white dust.

The sky was crystal blue. On the ground, there was no sign

of yidoh, sand leeches, bigmouths, or any other of the nefarious denizens of Nospherus that might have appeared to hinder his progress. Perhaps this was because of the moss-juice that the Sem had slathered on both horse and rider. Yet Guin knew that once the sun set the dangers would multiply and the going was sure to get rougher. This made it all the more critical that he cover as much distance as possible before then, while the sun still shone in the sky. Rinda had told him to cross over the Dog's Head, but even from atop a dune, he could not spot the oddly shaped landmark; he hoped to reach a vantage point from which he could see the mountain before the darkness fell.

And so Guin had ridden without rest. Frequently, he would slow to an amble so that he would not exhaust his mount, or dismount and walk alongside the horse. At these times he would pull some dried meat from his saddlebags and chew it slowly. After he felt his strength return, he would mount and crack his whip and they would be off at a gallop once more.

Only one time before now had he taken pause in his rugged advance. This was when he spied a black smear on the far southeastern horizon, so small that he thought it might be a trick of the eye—until it began to widen and he was able to make out the shapes of countless mounted riders. He was nowhere near where he expected to find the Lagon, and he was certain that he would not be so fortunate as to encounter them so soon, so he reasoned that what he saw was none other than the main Mongauli army on the move.

Quickly then he had jumped down from his mount and turned the horse away from the moving army so that they cast a slimmer profile against the dunes. Then, leading the stallion by the reins, he had walked on very slowly, careful not to raise any dust. His time was too precious to use up laying in wait for the danger to pass, but he knew that even across the distance that divided him from the Mongauli, nothing could stand out more clearly than the dark blotch of a mounted rider against the bleached canvas of Nospherus. Thankfully, it seemed that the invaders were moving too fast to spend much time looking around them. In their wake, a great gray cloud of dust rose and spread and at last dispersed like smoke from a campfire blown in the wind. Guin had not remounted until the Mongauli were so far off that there was no longer any danger of his being seen.

After that, he had ridden hard to make up for the time lost. The desert was featureless once more. No mirage-like armies of Mongauli or Lagon broke the even line of the horizon, and it felt as though no matter how far he went he was trapped forever in the same place.

Guin had no definite destination in mind. Had it not been for Rinda Farseer's oracular advice, he would not even be heading east now. Yet he was painfully aware that this journey was a great gamble, and that his time was limited. He had promised the Sem he would return on the fourth day, and already most of the first day had been spent in what felt at times like fruitless meandering across the sand. But a promise was a promise, and not only the fate of the Sem tribes, but the lives of Rinda and Remus, the holy twins of Parros, hung on his success in making good his word.

Still, Guin was not worried—or at least he showed no outward sign of concern. He knew that no amount of fretting about his chances would help him. Yet a dark look did come into his yellow eyes when, with the Dog's Head still not in sight, he noticed the gathering cloud of the sandstorm appear on the horizon.

For a while he forced himself to ignore the coming storm, and he urged his horse onward, plying his whip more forcefully than before. His mount sped tirelessly across the sand. At last, standing in the saddle of the galloping horse, Guin peered over his shoulder at the towering cloud and saw that it had now grown into a full-fledged maelstrom, much larger than before and trailing a dark ragged tail behind it. That could only mean it was coming toward him, and fast.

Still he showed no fear. He whipped the horse and galloped onward, as though to outrace the storm. If some great being such as Jarn had been watching from on high, Guin would have seemed no more than a frail and tiny speck, hardly moving across the endless white desert, pursued by a huge and angry growth, an animate black tumor that raged across the sand with the roar of a stampede. Ahead of the devouring storm, the flitting mote that was Guin would have looked almost powerless, his advance hopelessly slow.

Yet advance he did. He would not stop for the savagery of nature, or for any greater force of fate. He would fight the storm alone if he had to, never quitting without a struggle. Tiny, but undaunted, wild and proud, he was the embodiment of an in-domitable will and a fighting spirit without equal.

But even as he fought for distance on the sand, the relent-less storm revealed its cruel strength. Steadily it gained on the rider. The whirling sand and wind brought a sudden rain of pebbles down on Guin, stinging his shoulders and his horse's flanks, heralding the onslaught of the storm. In an instant, the clear blue of the sky turned a dark ashen hue. As though to echo the turmoil of the heavens, the sea of sand around Guin began to boil crazily as the denizens of Nospherus burst out of hiding and ran, flew, or slithered for their lives, trying in vain to escape the oncoming cataclysm.

When the cold blast of the wind flattened his ears against his leopard head, Guin finally stopped his horse. "Too dangerous to go further now," he muttered to himself, "I need to find some shelter…" Hurriedly he looked around, keeping a firm grip on the reins. Suddenly, his eyes shone with surprise.

"The Dog's Head!"

There, to the east, sat the giant canine form of the legendary mountain, hunched and black on the horizon. It was as though the desert had been hiding it from him, but now the veil had been lifted. Yet even as he gazed upon his goal the wind howled around him with renewed fury. With a deafening roar a sudden mighty gust forced the air out of his lungs and knocked him flat upon the ground. The sandstorm had arrived.

2

"Knights of Mongaul, halt!"

"Post the sentinels! The rest of you—at ease!"

The massive Mongauli host ground to a stop, the dust of its passage drifting around it. None among the invaders could have guessed how close they were to the main force of the Sem, sheltered at the oasis only a short distance from the scarred flats of the Devil's Anvil.

"A sandstorm is brewing. The sky has clouded." Amnelis frowned and peered at the roiling clouds racing over the horizon. "Gajus, what direction will the weather take?"

"It does not appear to be moving toward us. Our troops should suffer no harm. Yet if these clouds portend a true wildlands storm, the desert dwellers will emerge in great numbers to harass us. Each troop should be warned."

Amnelis frowned again. She lifted her bottomless green eyes and cast a suspicious gaze over the rolling white swells of the sea of sand. "This land is cursed," she spat. "I swear it moves against us." Once the storm-darkness came, the host would not be able to advance safely without the risk of riding into the midst of another colony of yidoh, or falling into the pit traps of the dread mouths-of-the-desert. Amnelis's face was calm, a picture of serenity, but beneath the surface she hid a growing frustration with their situation and impatience with their marked lack of progress. "There is a chance that the Sem will raid under cover of the storm. Warn the captains."

"Yes, my lady."

"We will be delayed again," she added in a mutter. "Still, we must find a way to make progress! We will reach the end of our supplies before long, and before that happens, I want very much to put an end to the Sem nuisance. These skirmishes get us nowhere." The general's voice rose again: "Gajus, we will choose a place to camp, send out scouts in all directions, and find the whereabouts of the Sem village. Then we will bring our main force to bear and crush them at their very root. That may be our best chance to end this quickly." Amnelis fingered the hilt of her sword, her thoughts roving inwardly. Her words were barely audible as she murmured to herself, "The villages of the Sem..."

"My lady? Did you say something?"

"We must find the Sem villages!"

"Of course, my lady."

"This *situation*..." the general's voice snapped out now again with barely contained fury, "this situation is unacceptable! How much time must we waste in dealing with monkeys—mere *monkeys*? I have a mission, a mission of utmost urgency upon which hangs the very fate of our mother Mongaul. I will not let a rabble of barbarian pygmies bar me from my destiny. Gajus!"

"Y-Yes, my lady!"

"We will hold a war council! Call the captains, raise the pavilion. I have decided that there is no need for us to sit and wait for the wildlings to bring the fight to us again. Why let them choose when and where we wage our war? It is Guin who hinders us, and Guin alone! The rest are just a mindless mob of monkeys!"

Gajus waited for Amnelis to finish her tirade, not daring to breathe. She didn't even look at him. Anger blazed in her eyes so brightly that the old diviner thought sparks might fly from them as she stared out across the darkening desert. The vast expanse of sand grew dusky, reflecting the oncoming storm. Her lips were drawn painfully taut. It seemed as though she had finally given herself leave to release the rage that she had kept buried deep inside. She was terrifyingly beautiful.

"My lady..."

"Gajus!" Amnelis suddenly raised a delicate fist and struck the knob of her saddle as if it were the catch to release a guillotine blade. "I can wait no longer. The wildlings must be destroyed.

I am thinking of two things only, Gajus. One, the Sem are like an overgrown hedge that must be cut off at its root. We will find their villages and stamp them into the ground. And next, we will take Guin's head and raise it high above our camp! I do not care who he is, nor what plan he brings to bear against us. His life is mine! Gajus, cast your stones! A divination, Gajus!"

"Yes, my lady."

The call went rapidly through the gathered host. "Orders! To war council! Orders!"

Amnelis sprang off her mount and cut across the newly established camp at a rapid pace, as though too impatient even to wait for the messengers to carry her orders for her. Her long white cloak flowed elegantly behind her and her golden hair sparkled like the shining palace of the ancient city of Nanto, while overhead the wasteland sky was fast turning the color of spilled ink. With her attendants in tow she strode toward the camp's center, and as she moved through each troop, the knights hurriedly dismounted and stepped aside to clear a way for her passage, then clutched their swords to their breasts in the Mongauli salute.

Amnelis paid them no attention at all.

I must have the head of Guin. When he is slain, the Sem will crumble. Why did I not realize this before? Amnelis reproached herself. Her heart was pounding, her breathing was shallow and her pace quickened. At that instant she wanted to leap on a horse at the head of her army and lead the charge herself.

"Orders! Orders!" the lady general shouted as she swept through the standing soldiers. "Pass the word for Feldrik and Irrim to report to me at once!"

Amnelis had left the diviner Gajus standing with his aged head bowed, a strange expression on his hooded face. There was an otherworldly glimmer in the caster's eyes as he watched the shining general stride away. When she was out of sight he quickly turned and lowered his gaze, hiding his face beneath his hood. "Raise my tent, bring my basin and divination board. Quickly!" he rasped to the attendants around him. Of all the men there, he knew best what would occur should there be any delay in his obedience to her request.

His entourage carried a tent just for occasions such as this, a simple affair consisting of four narrow poles and a black cloth that could be quickly drawn over them. It took but a moment for the caster's men to erect it. Then the leader among them, a dark-skinned man from Kravia, laid a mat beneath the tent's dark folds, upon which he spread gold dust in the shape of a pentagram. Finally he lit a stick of incense, then pushed out the other servants as Gajus came hurrying in and took his place upon the mat.

A short while later the caster emerged, looking flustered. He called out to Cal Moru of Kitai who was sitting perfectly still in his saddle nearby. "Master Cal Moru! Please, a moment of your time. The basin, you must come see the basin," Gajus croaked, a shudder in his voice.

The eastern mage, risen from the dead but not entirely alive, dismounted and moved his crippled body into the caster's tent. Inside, Gajus was pointing at the water basin and the divination board set beneath it.

"What's this?" Cal Moru rasped, his voice harsh in the caster's ears. "Remarkable!"

"Reluctant though I am to admit it, I have never seen a pattern so strange in all my years," Gajus murmured, profound unease overcoming his professional pride. "I know not whether it portends good or ill—or indeed whether it offers any prophecy at all!"

"It cannot be an omen of good. Look. Here, this is our army. And in our army, a star of fire! It portends disaster and...and a lasting legacy, at the same time."

"But what legacy is that?"

"Master Gajus, in the east, where my country lies, when there is a single star that bears two meanings, they say it foretells a coming revolution. But what this means for our army, I cannot say."

"It is clear that some sort of great and uncommon change is about to come to the army of Mongaul. But how to report this to the lady general?"

"The shining star spills its light!" Cal Moru's bony fingertip shook as he pointed at the divining board. "The light flows to the east. There is a magnetism in the east, yes, and this causes the shining star to go wild!"

"We do know why," Gajus said softly. "The lady general is obsessed with this leopard-man, more than she knows. She trembles when she says the half-beast's name, and she becomes all the more vexed as she seeks to hide her emotion." The aged caster traced the grooves of the divining board with his finger. "But this is *fate* that we see here. We cannot speak to her and hope that the light will change its course."

"All moves according to fate," Cal Moru intoned slowly. "Yet…"

"Yet?"

"There are many stars come to this land of Nospherus, and all of them play a great and powerful role in the shaping of fate. The fabric of power as made by the golden laws—the sacred division of things as they should be—has been stretched and made misshapen."

"Where, then, is the source of the power that works this change on us?"

"I do not know. However..." Cal Moru chuckled deep in his throat. "Master Gajus, we, too, are but patterned threads in this woven cloth."

"True enough. But this star of fire that we see here, I must know what it signifies. It troubles me deep in my bones."

"It is troubling indeed. And mysterious. Yet I believe we cannot behold its true nature, for it is like a seed in which the tree lies sleeping. Only when it breaks the surface of the earth at last will we see its destined shape."

"Yes, perhaps. But early this morning, during my usual readings, I saw no such star in our camp..."

The two mages lingered around the divining board and the alabaster basin, talking on in low voices as the water in the basin continued to swirl in a strange silent maelstrom. Outside, the wind was rising, shaking the black cloth of the diviner's tent and the gold star that decorated its side.

"At last!"

"Finally, it's our turn to bring the fight to them!"

The knights spoke eagerly amongst themselves. Seeing Amnelis striding through the ranks and hearing her messengers give the call to a council of war had an electrifying effect on the Mongauli, sending ripples of activity through the troops. Being constantly at the mercy of their enemies, always waiting for the next raid, had rotted away their morale. But whispered rumors run fast, and now they knew that their lady general intended to lead them to a decisive victory. The aggravating skirmishes would finally be over, ended by a pitched battle in which the knights could show their true strength. They felt their warriors' pride stir once again.

"If we brought the full force of our army to bear on them, even once, those wildlings wouldn't stand a chance!" boasted one of the knights.

"If we'd just gone on the attack earlier, we might not have lost Viscount Leegan," another observed glumly.

"'Ey, there's no call to doubt past strategy," the first replied.

"He's right," a third added. "I'm sure everything up until now has been some plan of the Lady Amnelis. She's always right."

Far behind them in the ranks, out of earshot of the knights, the footsoldiers, too, fell out of formation and exchanged theories about a change in fortune.

"Say, if we can massacre these Sem, 's a good bet we'll be headin' back home, 'tis."

"Awh, only if we've the luck to live, *and* we do our duty, *and* we get assigned with the homecomin' troops n' not stationed out in Doal's Nowhere."

"I want t' go home somethin' awful. I've had me fill o' these wildlings and this sand."

"Ye stop yer whinin' now. Cap'n hears you and you'll get a whippin' fer sure."

"Aye, and I'd welcome it gladly! Sand, sand, n' more sand! Let's have at these Sem and get back quick t' the glorious green on the *other* side o' the Kes."

"When a man says stop yer whinin' it don't mean ye should go shoutin', now! Quiet, or there'll be hell to pay fer all of us."

"Aah, I'll bet they're just harvestin' the vasya fruit back in Odain…"

The sandstorm was approaching. While it looked as though the brunt of it would miss the Mongauli, the wind had picked up considerably, and although the hour was still early it had grown quite dark. The Gohrans could hear the howling of desert wolves on the wind, and see sand worms burrowing under the dunes and desert lizards scampering away as fast as they could run. Wisps of angel hair began an unsettling pale dance in the swirling sands that rose in the whistling gusts. Stalks of desert worm-wood—one of the few plants that grew in the wastes—were pulled roots and all from the sand and came flying among the knights, slapping against their faces and then blowing away over their heads and off into the sky. It seemed that the Nospherus desert had finally decided to rescind any and all grace it had shown the human interlopers; it had bared its true face, bloodthirsty and mercilessly cruel.

"I don't believe it! This bleedin' wasteland *can* get worse!" moaned the footsoldier who had just been pining for his home in Odain.

"'Tis a land forsaken by the gods," his companion agreed.

"If I'd known 'twas this bad, I'd have gladly paid a fine to get out o' duty. *Any* fine."

"Could be even worse, yet," the other observed philosophically, squinting his eyes against the fine grit blowing in the wind as he gazed suspiciously out into the gathering darkness. "Just think what would happen if the Sem attacked us now."

Fear of attack was a concern the leaders of the army also shared.

"Preparations for the war council are complete, my lord," Garanth reported to Count Marus.

The count turned to him with a face that was filled with concern. "The timing could be no worse. At last, the Lady has decided to strike back, and now *this.*" He waved a hand toward the swirling murk of the approaching storm. "Even the skies in this land are the ally of the Sem."

"This is their land, after all."

Garanth turned to see who had spoken to the count so lightly. It was Eru of Troop Argon. In a very short time, the young knight had become the favorite of the aged count. It was perhaps his resemblance to Count Marus's son, far away in the capital, that first moved the count to pick him for his personal guard; yet there was something in this spirited, almost impetuous youth's manner that had also made many others like him. And trust him.

"Of course, since we cannot move while the storm is on, now is a perfect time to hold the council. We can march as soon as the weather clears," Garanth noted, hoping to ease the count's worries. "I am sure that the lady general plans an all-out attack this time. Something that will put an end to this sorry business with the Sem for good."

"Indeed I hope that is what she intends. If not, then I will suggest such a strategy myself." Count Marus brushed the dust off the sleeves of his cloak and readied himself for the meeting. "Now, let us not keep the Lady waiting. Wouldn't want her to lose her temper, would we, Garanth?"

"If a general attack is planned, let it be our corps that spearheads the assault, Captain," Eru interjected, a hint of mischief sparkling in his eyes. "The men are eager to hunt Sem."

"As am I!" Marus responded. He nodded, and favored Eru with a look as fond as if the young man were his own son or grandchild. "Perhaps I *shall* request that we be allowed to lead the attack." So saying he set off with Garanth toward the hastily erected pavilion.

The knights and footsoldiers had plenty to do, preparing for the decisive battle that they all hoped was near even as they maintained a watch for any signs of a possible Sem raid under cover of the storm. The number of sentries was doubled, and they clanked in their armor as they walked the perimeter, scanning in all directions for any hint of the wildlings.

Through the commotion, Astrias, with Pollak in tow, Tangard, Irrim, Feldrik, and the other officers filed into the pavilion behind Count Marus. Every face glowed with martial spirit. Finally, they would be allowed to awaken from the lethargic routine of defense and counterattack. Eager to hear the general's words, they assembled quickly; then the door flap of the pavilion was lowered and sealed, and the council of war began.

The wind howled, and the angel hair came in greater quantities, until the light flurry had become a steady fall. Through the swirling dust, messengers ran back and forth, delivering orders.

"The sandstorm comes!"

"Soldiers, use your cloaks when the wind starts hurling stones! Raise them over your faces, and keep low behind the horses."

"Sentries, don't face into the wind with your faceplates up, or the sand will take your eyes!"

"Don't let the Sem catch you unawares. Ears and eyes open

at all times! Vigilance!"

"The storm will last only a *twist*. Do not leave your posts. Feed your mounts and conserve your strength."

"No one leave the formation!"

Eru was unconcerned with the orders. Standing with his cloak drawn close and his hood pulled all the way up, he watched a page taking care of Count Marus's favorite steed, then leisurely made his way back to his own horse. Reaching into a small pocket under his saddle, he pulled out a sheet of parchment. Quickly, then, in the shadow of his horse, he drew out a stylus and began to write.

In a moment he was finished. Satisfied, he drew back his hood and looked around.

"What's this? You, what are you writing there?"

He had thought no one was watching him, but as he stepped out from behind his steed, he realized that he was wrong. The lieutenant from the guard troop to which he now belonged had taken an interest in the new arrival. Eru jumped up, startled.

"N-Nothing! It's nothing. I...am a bit of a poet, see. I write poetry. Lyrics really. I was thinking of putting some words about this here sandstorm to a kitara tune, maybe make a ballad of sorts." Eru's excuses tumbled hastily and he nervously licked his lips. The color rose in his dusky face.

The lieutenant questioned him no further, however. His

attention had drifted toward the pavilion in the center of the formation where the war council was under way. Eru, flustered, folded the sheet of parchment and tucked it under his armor. Then he swiftly dug out a gati ball and some vasya fruit and bit into them, munching rapidly—to all appearances wholly occupied with eating.

The wind grew steadily stronger. The blobs of angel hair were like countless white ghosts flying among the Mongauli, and the dried wormwood branches made a dry slapping sound against their armor. The clouds were low and dark, and the invaders could see the giant storm cyclone moving past them in the distance, toward the east. Each knight and soldier knew that getting caught in that terrible whirlwind would have meant their end, and they shivered in their armor and thanked Jarn for turning it aside, one gift of fate in this accursed place. Even as they watched, the cyclone was growing, becoming more monstrous. It ripped up sand, plants, stones, everything living or dead that lay in its path, and carried all upwards in a fearful maelstrom of wind. It was the will of Doal Demongod incarnate, bringing a message to those who trespassed in his domain.

Then the edge of the true storm swept over the encampment.

It did not rain in dry Nospherus. Instead, the storm seemed to suck the moisture from everything it touched. Furiously its savage winds beat upon the land, and the sand and pebbles they carried scoured stone and steel and skin.

This was the moment for which the bizarre and fearful Marches creatures that had lain hidden in the path of the advancing army had been waiting. Innumerable cries and vengeful howls mingled suddenly with the screeching of the wind, and a sound of weeping, too, that sent chills up the spine of every Mongauli man there. The sand boiled and shook, white tentacles erupting from below the surface to grab unlucky sentries to drag them down into a grit-filled grave. Their screams and curses and prayers to the gods were lost in the roar of the storm. Nospherus had revealed its inmost nature, and it was red in tooth and claw.

3

Had Guin made a hasty decision to attempt to escape the sandstorm, had he misjudged his shelter even slightly, then surely he and all the power of fate that carried him would have fallen before the might of the sandy tempest. But Guin—creature of mystery that he was, with no memory of his life before the day he appeared in the Roodwood beneath Stafolos Keep—possessed an uncanny instinct for survival that so far had steered him true through every peril he encountered.

It did not fail him now. The instant he felt the touch of the sandstorm's assault at his back, he leapt from his horse and, jerking powerfully on the reins, pulled the beast down beside him so that its body shielded him against the wind. Then he curled up like an infant, drawing up his knees and wrapping both arms protectively around his head.

A hail of sand and pebbles hurtled down upon him, making dry slapping sounds as they bounced off the cloak that shrouded his massive frame. Above the racket, Guin could just make out the mournful whinnying of the horse...and then all was lost in a fury of noise as the storm rushed over them.

The keening howl of the wind transformed into a sound like rolling thunder. Guin closed his eyes and kept his hands up for protection. Then the noise of thunder became a high, ripping scream, and Guin felt as if impossibly giant, violent hands had snatched him up from his shelter and were tossing him about. Suddenly he had the eerie sensation that he had been cast into a white void, a vacuum of space in the midst of the storm. He could hear strange sounds in the wind—whimpering and sobbing—and the light against his tightly closed eyelids changed from a perfect blackness to a blaze of white.

Ferocious nature had made the whole of the desert its domain, and it lusted for destruction. The cyclone swept up all before it in its million fists and shook earth, sand, and solid rock until all were broken, fragmented like porcelain dolls tossed in an iron box. The ricocheting of stone against stone and sand against sand mixed with the crackling sound of the cyclone's takings being sucked into the vacuum at its center.

Even the beast-god Cirenos himself would not have survived long in that storm without injury. The black tentacles of the maelstrom swirled high into the cloud-filled sky, and again and again the cyclone struck at the earth with a hammer of air, transforming the vast desert into a boiling storm-sea. It was as if Zortho, the great, blind, Doal-spawned serpent of the underworld, had fallen into a black rage and burst up through the foundations of the world, the span of his giant body seething with a craving for destruction that sent him writhing and twisting across the tortured earth. Nospherus bowed its cursed body before the wrath of Doal. The ground shivered with every breath and trembled at every cry of rage.

A dense wall of seething air, saturated with sand and rock, rose higher and higher into the skies and stained them black as pitch. The cyclone sucked the sand upwards and threw it at the heavens, along with the hapless yidoh, sand leeches, and mouths-of-the-desert that had sought refuge by tunneling underground. In its wake the whirling tempest left a series of broad crevasses filled with savagely pitted holes, like graveyards robbed of all their corpses and left open to the sky; yet each gaping pit was exposed for mere instants before the roiling rivers of sand that flowed behind the vortex came in a landslide from three sides to fill it. This storm was an explosive power of the kind that made men believe that the end of the world—Armageddon—was coming. No strength, no knowledge, no amount of preparation could protect a mere mortal from the direct assault of that power.

The sandstorm raged for a *twist* that seemed to last an eternity. It was a storm of rare proportions, a true great cyclone, visible from as far away as the guardroom at Alvon Keep on the other side of the Kes River. There, the keep-lord Count Ricard stood on the watchtower, fretting about the wellbeing of the expeditionary army, and he could not be persuaded to leave. He had seen the reports coming from the signal fires: earlier that day, further down the Kes, desert wormwood, a plant known to grow only in the deep interior of Nospherus, had been seen falling in the cultivated fields of the homesteaders near Tauride Castle.

Count Ricard paced back and forth. *This storm is the work of Doal and none other.* Nospherus was the demons' land, forgotten by the gods, and all its charity toward man had been spent. The storm was proof enough of that. Even above Alvon the sky was gray, and the earth shook and thudded as though Gloch's mares of legend were galloping back and forth across the distant desert.

By the time that the cyclone disappeared off into the hills in the northeast and the wind quieted to a sorrowful moan, the sun had long since set.

Guin dreamed.

He had lost consciousness in the violence of the storm, buffeted and tossed by the mighty winds. He was at the mercy of the cyclone, but even as his body succumbed, his spirit journeyed in the dream world, knowing not whether the things he saw were revelations from some higher being or mere empty illusion, the hallucinations at the edge of death.

All he knew was that there, in the midst of the storm and the ground-shaking stampede of Gloch's mares, he could hear a voice—horribly clear though from incredibly afar—calling his name:

Guin... Guin...

At first, he thought it was nothing more than the whine of the wind playing tricks on his ears.

Guin... Guin...

The voice grew stronger and more distinct. It crept into the void of his mind and circled like a moth around a lantern flame. Guin tried to answer.

Who are you? Why do you call me?

Guin... Guin... Guin!

Yes, I am Guin! I am here! WHO ARE YOU?

Guin...

The voice drew nearer, and then receded back into the distance. At times it seemed to mock him. At other moments, it seemed suddenly full of rage; it would thunder and become terrible and imperious. Only one thing about the voice did not change, and of this Guin was absolutely certain: it was that of a young woman.

But whether it was one woman who called to him, or many women, one after the other, he could not tell. It seemed to him that the speaker knew something of great importance that she sought to tell him. He knew that if he could just find out what that something was, if he could understand the message that was offered and yet withheld, then all would be made well, and he would be enveloped in a divine light of mercy and forgiveness.

I...

Guin tried vainly to move his mouth and scream aloud. He wanted to get the attention of the unknown speaker, to win her favor.

I know you! You are connected to me... I...was searching for you. There is something I must ask...something you must tell me! Why am I like this...why have I become...

Why have I

Why have

Why...

Guin was perplexed. He wanted to ask why he had become something, but what? What was the question he had to ask her? Why couldn't he remember?

I am

I am

I...

All around him was abruptly quiet. He was in a cavern, dark
and deep, a hollow place from which radiated a vast network of
caves and passages. Guin's thoughts echoed around him, racing
down tunnels and bouncing off hard, stone walls, multiplying
into infinity. "Stop playing games and show yourself!" he
shouted in anger. He could sense that the one he sought was
somewhere in these caves.

Show yourself

Show

Show...

The echo-voice sounded like that of a priest, reading the
divine oracles at the temple of Jarn.

Guin looked around. Neither torch nor lantern lit the cave,
but it was not completely dark, for the surface of the stone itself
was luminescent, and wherever he stepped, his feet left glowing
prints behind him. He felt certain that this place was somewhere
that he knew—that he had known. He had been here before,
perhaps many times. The floor and ceiling with their many protruding stalactites and stalagmites, and the damp, dark passages
that gaped on all sides, beckoning to him, were all terribly familiar; he felt nostalgic.

What was this place?

Guin tried to remember, but it seemed that the hands of

his memory were bound so fast that he could not even reach toward understanding; he could not even remember what it was he
knew he didn't know. He clutched the hilt of his beloved sword,
still hanging at his waist, and drew it with a flourish. The depth
of trust and security that he felt when he ran his hand along the
supple steel of its blade surprised him and gave him a new confidence. "With this," he said to the cave walls, "I will meet any
plan, any challenge you have laid for me. Do what you will, I
care not."

He sheathed the weapon again, making certain that it was
loose in its scabbard so that he would be able to draw it in an instant if necessary. Then he set out to explore the caves, seeking
to find whatever it was that he must find, wherever it was that he
must go.

Suddenly his entire body felt leaden with fatigue. The gloom
that afflicts the traveler on a tremendous journey clouded his
heart, and the feel of the thick, humid air seemed to slow his
every movement. He drew his sword again and peered around
warily, steeling his thoughts to cut through the torpor that
threatened to fill his limbs and strand him here.

The branching side passages of the cave had seemed innumerable at first, but on closer examination he found that there
were only four main passages leading away from where he stood.
He was at a crossroads of sorts. All the other openings dead-

ended quickly, or fed into one of the four larger tunnels. These alone lay open, one in each direction, like dark, toothless mouths waiting to devour him.

He thought to himself for a while about which path to take. He felt strangely hesitant about choosing any of them; he wanted to know what lay inside them *before* he made his choice, yet he knew that that would be impossible. Somehow he understood that the moment he learned what lay down a passage, it would change into something entirely different.

A thought came to him and he fished in the pocket of his waistband and withdrew a single coin. He would toss it in the air, and take the passage closest to where it landed. But when he looked closer at the coin, he froze.

The profile on the face of the small copper coin was that of a leopard-headed man. It was himself! But something was different. It took him a moment to realize what it was, but then he saw: above the relief of the leopard-furred head with open mouth and staring eyes was the shining crown of a king.

The crown was resplendent with many jewels and graced with a complex pattern of engraving. Surely it was the proud and noble symbol of the king of a mighty nation, steeped in tradition, glorious and strong.

What's this?

Guin's hand trembled slightly. He held the coin up and

peered at it for a long while. After a time he saw that around his miniature portrait there were runic letters inscribed in a circle.

"Proclaimed High King in the name of Janos, the Two-Faced God"... High King...?

Guin hurriedly turned the coin over. On the reverse side was another bust in relief, this one not of Guin, but of a woman. Her face was young and beautiful. Her hair was elegantly arranged above her head, and her small chin was turned slightly away. She was slender—her exquisite features spoke of a noble bloodline—but in the turn of her chin Guin saw stubbornness, a hardness of spirit. A royal crown sat above her braided hair, too, of the same design as Guin's but smaller. There were words below the relief.

"King Guin's Queen by the Guidance of Jarn"... King Guin's...queen? Guin gasped. *Queen? Who is this woman? What does this all mean?*

Guin stared at the strange coin that seemed to foretell his future rise to the throne, and his future queen, wondering when and how it had gotten into his pocket. He decided to save it and ponder its mysteries later, and he looked for another coin to throw. This time his fingers found the familiar shape of a raan tenthpiece, in common circulation throughout the Middle Country. Somewhat relieved, he flicked the second coin into the air with a quick snap of his thumb.

The coin arced high above his head then fell to his right, between him and the second opening to the right of where he stood.

"Very well," Guin muttered. He picked up the coin. Straightening his garb and gear, and sheathing his sword, he marched into the passage with long, incautious strides. For a moment as he went he considered whether or not he should mark his passing on the cave wall so that he would be able to find his way back, but soon decided that, since he had no idea where here was anyway, nor why he was here, there was little reason to do so.

As long as I go straight and keep going, I will arrive somewhere, he thought to himself, slowing down to navigate over the suddenly slippery rock floor. Everything still felt so familiar, yet this was an unsettling place nonetheless, a strange, malign subterranean road.

At times the tunnel he walked resembled the dark passage that brings us into life, and at others, the lightless realm between this world and the next, that we all must travel on the way to the Judgment, where the value of our lives and our souls is weighed on Jarn's scales. From time to time he saw pale lights in the distance, and he would stop, expecting them to be will o' the wisps, or the glimmering souls of the dead; then they would disappear once more, leaving nothing behind but silence.

Guin did not look back. He knew not to. Somehow, he knew that if he looked and saw the place from which he had come, he would have done something wrong that he could not take back.

The hair on the back of Guin's neck bristled, and it seemed that some sense beyond the ordinary five was telling him which tunnels held the true path, and which were false ways that led to danger. As he walked, the air behind him became thicker and darker, denying him a way back.

Suddenly he heard a voice laughing evilly behind him, like a desert hyena or a simperwolf. But he did not turn around to look.

The other voice that he had heard earlier, calling his name, had ceased completely. He took the paths that he felt to be right and willed himself not to think about what might happen were he to choose incorrectly. Those who were led by fate and not chance, those who, all the while believing there was only chance, invariably did what must be done and chose the right course—ironically, only such ones were of any use to destiny. Fate and chance, the two faces of a single head, illuminated the world; to which of them a man reached out determined whether he was to be a helmsman or a galley slave.

Enfolded and protected by the cavern darkness, Guin felt oddly safe. He was awake, but not awake, he was born yet unborn, and in this was strange calm and physical repletion.

This is the path we walk, he thought. *Most of our souls will only partly awaken. Even the ones called sages are nothing more than tired men blinking their drowsy eyes in the gloom. We are born sleeping, and we walk in a deep dream throughout our lives. Our heads rise slowly, only to settle back on our pillows— life is just a brief tossing and turning that barely disturbs our slumber. Then we return to sleep, an eternal sleep from which we will never awaken. Who is truly awake? Who rules the border between reality and dream? Who rolls the die of chance and weaves the fabric of our fate? The gods? What are gods; where are they? Why have they chosen me? Who am I? For what have I lifted my head from its ancient slumber?*

Who am I…?

Guin swallowed. Rounding a shallow bend, he saw that the endless dark path before him had led him to a secret at last. Not far ahead, now, a pale uncertain form of light broke the shadows. Facing this light, Guin put his hand on the hilt of his sword and began to run, careful to watch his step. Now the darkness seemed to resist his advance; heavy and cloying, it clung about his neck and dragged at his straining limbs.

That light!

The pale bluish-white light seemed to emanate from a body lying directly across his path up ahead. There was a step down, and the tunnel widened to a room. Guin kept a firm grip on his sword and, slowing, carefully approached.

When he finally got close enough to see the source of the light for what it was, he stopped abruptly and a low growl spilled from his mouth: "What is this?"

The thing Guin looked down upon was strange indeed. It appeared to be an enormous, palely glowing infant almost as large as Guin himself. It had no arms or legs and was curled up like a caterpillar, a great lump of flesh with a giant head and giant torso.

Then—it turned to look at him!

"Hrrgah!"

For all his courage, Guin could not contain a yelp of surprise, and he leapt back. The infant had but a single giant eye in the middle of its swollen head, and the moment it opened this eye to gaze upon him a tremendous blazing brilliance surrounded Guin and filled the chamber. The walls glowed like flowing lava, as bright as if the leopard-man stood in the crater of an erupting volcano.

Find your own path...

In the middle of that explosion of light, Guin heard a new voice entirely different from the ones before. It was a man's voice, sounding far away, yet strong, deeply resonant. After a moment Guin surmised that it was coming from the mouth of the limbless baby before him, though he knew the words did not originate in any throat, lungs, or lips, but in a higher organ without form.

You must walk your own path, meet your own fate. Crush crown and chains alike. Three will guide you, women all...

"Three women?" Guin shouted.

One will show you your fate... One will show you your crown... And one will show you yourself.

"Who are these women? No—who am I! Why do I look the way I do? Am I under some mage's spell? Tell me, how is a man who does not even know his own past supposed to find the true path to his future?"

You will find it... the resonant voice's answer rang harsh and cold in Guin's ears. *For you are not a man.*

"Not a...what?!" Guin howled. He was filled with frustrated rage, and another powerful emotion that he did not understand: he was afraid.

"If I am not a man, what am I? A mere beast? A monster? Tell me—if I am not a man, then why was I given a man's life? Why am I here?"

Heed, the voice answered, *you are not a man...yet. Find your path, find the three, become who you were meant to be.*

"How will I find them? Where must I go?"

You must walk the true path.

"How do I know which way that is? How do I know which women are the three?"

Guin... Guin!

It was the young woman's voice that had called to him in the storm.

Guin jumped in surprise, then whirled around to see a woman's silhouette, black and featureless in the incandescence of the cavern. She was reaching a hand out towards him. She was trying to give him something.

"Is she one of the three?" Guin shouted and charged towards her. The silhouette faltered, apparently frightened. She turned lightly and began to run away from him.

"Wait!" Guin ran with long strides, quickly closing the distance between them.

With his powerful hands he grabbed the woman. She screamed and tried to pull away. The soft feel of her shoulders and her slender neck made the blood rise to Guin's face. "Is this her? Will she give me my fate, my crown, or my own self? Will she bring me from this purgatory into the world of men?"

Sharply Guin pulled the woman toward him. Her long swirling hair flowed across her face, concealing her features. The brilliance surrounding them filled her, turning her locks into threads of gleaming light, so that try as he might he could not be certain of their true color. Guin pushed aside the hair that wrapped around his fingers and turned her face towards his. Then he screamed.

"You!"

Everything tumbled into darkness. All light faded, all the world crumbled, all reality dissolved. Guin fell headfirst into a bottomless void, his mind filled with her shining smile.

—— 4 ——

The wind that coursed along Guin's bared skin was cool and pleasant. To one lately accustomed to the dry inferno that reigned in the desert, the wind felt as refreshing as a plunge into cold water after a long day in the sun. A low, satisfied growl came unbidden from his lips, and he stretched his curled limbs. Then his right hand brushed against something hard and he felt the sting of an open cut across his fingers. The pain dragged him out of his half-sleep to full wakefulness. Reflexively, Guin sprang to his feet with a warrior's speed, then sank into a fighting crouch. His eyes darted, scanning the surroundings.

"What in Doal's name?"

When the sandstorm lifted him, he had surrendered his body to the forceful winds' assault and his fate to the gods. He had known that if and when he woke again there was no telling where he would find himself. Even so, this place defied all his expectations.

"Is this Nospherus?" Guin's voice dropped to a dubious whisper. Even in the darkness that surrounded him he could see that, Nospherus or not, he was certainly nowhere near the desert where he had begun the day.

"And what is this?" he muttered, reaching down a hand to touch the ground upon which he had lain. It was hard and cold, and slightly damp—a sandless, rocky terrain. He had wakened himself when his hand struck one of the giant boulders that lay all around him. The cold stone was slick with nighttime dew, and in its shade a damp moss was growing thickly. Even without close inspection, Guin could tell that the moss was entirely different from the desiccated lichens of the desert.

"My horse..." He looked around. His mount was nowhere to be seen. Slowly, he straightened and began a careful self-inspection to make sure he was in one piece. He seemed to have suffered innumerable abrasions over his entire body, and his pitted skin tingled with the pain, as if he had taken a long bath in a steaming tub of hot peppers. Yet he was relieved to find that he had suffered no serious injuries, no fracture or sprain that might slow him down.

My sword... Guin put his hand to his waist. *Gone.*

He looked around with shining eyes, but the heavy blade that he had worn was nowhere to be seen. *Was I carried here while I slept by some sandflow pushed by the storm? Here, to these rocky hills?*

He thought it entirely impossible. Other than the tortuous crags in the northeast where the Sem made their home, and perhaps some other outcrops in the unknown depths of Nospherus, all of the land between the Kes and the Kanan Mountains was a sea of sand. Furthermore, the place where Guin had encountered the sandstorm was right in the middle of that barren sea, only a half-day out of the oasis. Yet by the dampness of the air these mountains would have to be deep in Nospherus indeed; and, no matter how fast the sand had been flowing, or how violently the cyclone had snatched him from the earth, he did not think either sand or wind was capable of carrying his giant body so far.

Yet, the rocks around him and the cold stars that twinkled in the night sky above him were real enough; indeed, the rocks' solid presence made the earlier storm seem, in contrast, like a dream.

Guin gave a wordless growl, and, choosing the highest of the boulders around him, he scrambled to its top, wary of hidden dangers as he went. Standing atop the great stone, he looked around in all directions. He growled again. Far below him he could see a wide, flat land, as smooth and flat as the calm sea.

Nospherus.

Then he lifted his head. Countless stars hung shining in the sky, so close it seemed as though he could reach up and touch them.

The Eye of Jarn...

Guin clenched a fist unconsciously as he scanned the sky for the Dawn Star, known as Jarn's Eye, which hung forever like a guiding lantern in the eastern sky. There it was: near the peak of the rocky mountain that rose directly before him.

I'm well to the east of where I was. Could this actually be the Dog's Head I'm standing on?

The mountain, with its peculiar canine silhouette, was one of the few clear landmarks in Nospherus, the highest peak in the Kanan range. On the near side of the featureless desert, the Sem used the Dog's Head for all navigation. Places were spoken of as being so many days' walk from Dog's Head, or to lie on the left or right hand of the mountain. It was their surest point of reference, anchored in the solid bedrock beneath the shifting sands of the desert. If the peak towering over him really was the Dog's Head, it meant that he had made it to the first waypoint of his journey.

But to be carried by the cyclone and wake up here, at the Dog's Head...

Guin clenched his fist again. Unsettling though it was, he had to admit that he felt the workings of a conscious mind, as if something more vast and powerful than any human will had chosen his destination for him and then called on unearthly forces to bring him there.

Something manipulates me—determines my every move! I am merely taking the steps proscribed for me...

The leopard-man's scarred body shivered. Fleetingly he recalled the bizarre dream that had come to him while he was lost in the storm. It was the kind of dream that seemed to be woven of the fabric of destiny itself—a dream that foretold change not just for Guin, but for the entire world. Yet this vague sense, of dire importance, was all that he could remember. All other details of the dream had been wiped clean from his mind.

He sighed and leapt down from the boulder. There were too many questions demanding answers that would never come, and he was more of a mind to make some progress in his journey than to sit in the wilderness contemplating the will of the heavens. To him and to those who cast their fate with him, the gods were very real, and very sacred. Trying in vain to understand their workings would have been an act of sacrilege.

In any case, he could sense that some higher power now desired him to seize the chance that was laid before him. Whether it was Janos Highgod, Jarn Fateweaver, or even Doal Demonlord himself, he did not know; but he felt that the gaze of a great being was upon him, and he was certain that this divine force was manipulating the events of his life, guiding him toward the fulfillment of his chosen role. The sandstorm, his miraculous transportation to the east, even his notion to seek the aid of the Lagon—all of these things could be but pieces of some higher being's plan.

If so, then what? Then all men are merely spiders, weaving a predetermined web of life...moving and spinning out their days as something else sees fit.

Guin looked up at the mountain, considering his options. If he could not divine the meaning of the journey laid out before him, he could at least speed it to its finish. He seemed to be positioned in a scree field on the western skirts of the peak. The silhouette of the summit above him was dark as a square of black silk against the starry sky. Like a flea on a dog's neck, he was too close to see whether he was perched upon the snout or the nape of the Dog's Head he had seen from the desert. But it was clear from the considerable elevation and the cool damp of the night air that he was high upon the mountain. The desert floor of Nospherus had looked impossibly far below when he had climbed the boulder to scout out his position, but if it were daytime, and if the winds were blowing favorably, he might have been able to see the far-off Kes, or even the sprawling green of Gohra beyond it.

East—Rinda had said "go east."

The revelations of the farseer echoed in his mind.

"Where the white stones dance upon the black mountain…
Beware the death-wind…"

At night, the mountain on which he stood was black enough. Perhaps he would find white rocks ahead, and perhaps the death-wind was the cyclone that had deposited him here. Though in retrospect the cyclone seemed more of a lifesaver than a death-wind for having carried him so far.

Sifting these thoughts, Guin began to wend his way through the field of boulders. Losing his sword was an unfortunate blow, and though he still could rely on his great strength, his body ached from the battering it had taken. The storm had also stolen his supply of food and water. All that remained to him was a sharp, slender dagger tucked into his waistband which had somehow avoided being torn away, and some small strips of dried fruit he had carried in his pocket. These were meager possessions for defending himself from attack or starvation.

Still, he thought, scrambling up rocks and jumping down into hollows, making his way where there was no path, *the horse would not have been much good in this terrain. And I've gotten through much worse before.*

Suddenly he stiffened, startled by his own thought. For a moment he had a peculiar sensation that his memory had returned. But when he focused, trying to recollect anything—an emotion, a face—that might belong to the years he must have lived before appearing by the pool in the Roodwood, he was confronted once again by an empty, answerless abyss.

Try as he might to reach back to his past, everything but his own name was a blank. All he had left from the earlier days of his life was a conviction that, no matter what difficulty afflicted him or what mighty foe stood against him, in the end he would prevail. Whether it was with his sword or with his two strong arms, leading a massive army or a small company of elites, he knew that he would overcome any obstacle, he would cut through to his destiny. He did not know this as one knows facts that are learned or stories that are told; rather, he felt it to be true. It was clear to Guin that he had experienced much in his life. But what possible chain of events could have led to his sudden appearance before the twins—and in such a strange guise?

This question had lingered as a deep unease at the back of his mind since he had first joined Rinda and Remus after his uncanny rebirth in the forest. The unease had stuck with him, despite his confidence in the survival instincts that had seen him through any number of difficulties already. This was the basic question at the axis of his existence.

What could be down there in the depths of my memory? What fearful, terrible secret? Am I better off not knowing?

Guin rubbed the short, dense fur on his forehead with his hand. His skull was rounded, with an arched nose, while many short whiskers surrounded a maw set with vicious fangs. *I have the head of a beast*, he reminded himself for the thousandth time.

Was this indeed the head with which he had been born, or had a mask been set over his true human face, or was this a transformation brought about by some curse, some weird power of magic? Even this he did not know—he had not even a hint as to the true reason. Yet he had a strange feeling that, despite all the bizarre tricks that fate had played upon him, there were some aspects of his life that had not been bound, that his role in the world was not completely decided.

As he remembered it now, when he first appeared in the Roodwood he had truly been like an infant. Not only had he been unable to talk, he could not even drink or eat, and when he had tried to do these things he had found it horribly difficult; even such simple actions had brought him much pain. But now he felt as though he had lived long years with this leopard head, and that with it he was a wholly natural being. He drank, ate, and spoke with no difficulty, and even knew the tongue of the Sem wildlings. It was almost as if the deity that watched over him was fixing his progress, making adjustments as it saw fit.

How else could he have known the weakness of the yidoh, the tactics of Alzandross, the basics of war and politics in the Middle Country? How else could he have been so highly skilled with the longsword, the spear, and the crossbow?

What am I? What is my purpose? Does something use me as its puppet, its avatar in this world, moving me according to its desires?

Surely something *does…but what?*

His thoughts had spun back to that central unanswerable question.

Do I have no limits? If something in heaven controls me, and I am only moving along a predetermined path, do I have no limits as a man? With my strength, my endurance, my power, my skill in battle, what can I do? What was I meant to achieve? Or perhaps I was meant to be nothing at all. Perhaps I was not supposed to be. Perhaps I would be better off dead.

Guin trembled. His thoughts now roamed into domains where the minds of men are unwise to stray. He knew well enough that he could answer that last question if he so wished. It would be as simple as drawing the dagger at his waist, or flinging himself from one of the many ledges around him. Then he would soon know if he was an immortal puppet or a living thing with freakish form fated to die. But the cruel irony was that, if indeed he was a mortal man with a will of his own, he would have to die to be certain of it, and his death would render the knowledge useless to him.

Guin shivered once more, tore his eyes away from his dagger, and uttered the name of Janos.

Testing the gods, testing one's own destiny, is the greatest of all sacrileges.

He shook his head like an animal shaking off water and put his frustrated introspections aside for another time. He had not stopped while he thought, his feet beating a steady, slow progress through the rocky terrain, and already he had covered a considerable distance. Hunger began to nip at his stomach, and thirst itched in his throat, but he feared eating what little he had too soon; and he felt no need for rest.

The cyclone had considerably reduced the length of his urgent journey. Still, there was no proof that the place of which Rinda had spoken, where the white rock danced with the black mountain, was where he expected to find it, on the other side of the Dog's Head. There was also the chance that, even should he find the Lagon, his pleas would go unheard. If he did manage to persuade them, there was no guarantee that the Sem would be able to hold out long enough for their arrival to make any difference.

With the odds as they were, an ordinary man might not have sought to undertake the journey at all. It was crazy—an unrealistic dream. But Guin spat even as this thought came to him. He was through with thinking, he decided. He would cross into the land beyond the Dog's Head and see what he could see. That was all he need think about.

His path now sloped upwards, continuing through terrain similar to that through which he had already traveled, damp shelves of stone strewn with loose boulders and rocks. The star-filled sky was close above his head. Even though this, too, was a part of Nospherus, its plants and animals were a world apart from those of the low-lying desert. No yidoh, no sand leeches, no bigmouths were here. All such beasts hid in the swells and lulls of the sandy sea below, making the white, dry, wind-blown desert their home, eking their bizarre lives out in its merciless hot climate. Many of them, from the bulbous yidoh to the tiny vampire flies and sprawling bloodmoss, specialized in sucking the blood and vital fluids of their prey. It was the easiest way to secure both water and nutrition in such a parched environment.

But, here in these rocks, the animals and plants lived lives that were much colder, although no less outwardly violent.

The moon came up and lit the ground at Guin's feet, making his way somewhat easier to find. He pressed on up the steepening slope at a rapid pace, still with breath to spare. For a while, nothing hindered his progress. Jarn's Eye shone high in the eastern sky, dozing far beyond Guin on his lone journey across Nospherus. In the endless sand-waves behind him were hidden the Sem camp at the oasis, and the night camp of the Mongauli. The desert was dark and silent, its calm face now showing no trace of so recently having been ravaged by the giant storm.

The gathering boulders closed in on either side of Guin's path. They were now close enough together that he decided he could move faster by jumping from boulder to boulder—a strategy that would also allow him to see more of the surrounding landscape. Eyeing a handhold on the rock face to his right, he reached out with his hand and stepped up—

Immediately Guin gave a short howl and jumped back down.

The boulder before him, which had seemed as cold and lifeless as all the others he had passed, had trembled warmly under his touch, and then come to life, reaching aggressively with stony pseudopods to grab at his outstretched hand.

His honed reflexes saved the leopard-man. He felt the warmth of the thing just as his hand was touching its surface, and leapt back, drawing the dagger from his waistband. A mouth opened in the rock-shape and lunged for him. Guin dodged aside, keeping his body well away from the reaching jaws, and plunged his dagger into the living boulder.

His blade hit something rubbery and unpleasant. But though the dagger cut deep, he could not tell whether the creature felt any pain at all.

For a third time, it came at him. This time he awaited its attack and, the very instant before it took him, lashed out with his right leg in a swift powerful kick to its underside. A stab of pain shot through his foot, but the living rock went flying upwards, split into two.

The bottom part rose only a few handspans before falling back to the ground with a hard thud. Guin eyed it warily, but it appeared to be no more than a normal rock. Meanwhile the upper half of the thing quickly lost its rounded shape, flattening into a sheet and spreading wide as it lifted higher in the air, then began to fall.

Guin's foot kicked the descending creature just before it hit the ground, flipping it up and over. It tried to wrap around his leg, but it was too slow, and it ended up falling to the ground upside down. There it lay spread out, its underbelly squirming with countless white thread-like pseudopods. They grasped at the air, undulating in nauseating pulses. Without hesitation Guin knelt and used his dagger to cut the revolting creature into strips.

As he cut, he grunted under his breath: "A stone-mimic." These were predators that used shapeshifting as camouflage. They lived by clinging motionless to the tops of boulders, looking just like their stony perches, until a hapless animal passed them by. Then they would seize and wrap around their prey, suffocating them even as they began to feed.

Guin muttered, "I don't suppose these are edible." He moved to put away his dagger, then suddenly tensed, ready for action. Some sixth sense was screaming danger.

His yellow eyes narrowed with suspicion, giving off a bestial light in the darkness. The hair rose on the back of his head and his feline nostrils flared. His upper lip drew back, baring long gleaming fangs, and an angry growl of warning sounded in his throat.

It was as though he had suddenly lost the half of him that was human and become, in an instant, a perfect and complete beast. Had some travelers come across him at just that moment, they would not have seen a man with the head of a great cat waiting there in the shadow. Rather they would have believed that they had stumbled across a giant, man-eating leopard, and the shock would have frozen them where they stood.

All the humanity had vanished from Guin's eyes. He growled, low and threatening, and an eerie wild howl answered him, followed by the ragged breathing of some creature.

Then through the gap between two boulders he saw a pair of eyes shining, burning red as ghost-fires. As he watched, they multiplied, two pairs, three pairs, until suddenly they were everywhere, in the shadows throughout the boulders, in the countless dips and hollows of the slope. It was as though he had blundered into a convocation of will o' the wisps.

Each pair of flames burned with a bloodlust that was unmistakable in its violence, savagely brightened by the cruel joy of the hunt. Ragged animal panting filled the night air, punctuated by short threatening growls. Then the musky stench of matted fur and bloody jaws assaulted Guin's senses. The creatures' voices closed in around him, changing now to short, excited breaths, filled with anticipation of the kill.

Guin moved swiftly to put a large boulder at his back. Then he stood without moving a muscle. His eyes flared with rage, as though he thought to defy all those demon-flames with his lone pair of fierce golden orbs.

His hand gripped his slender dagger tightly. For a moment he felt an acute chagrin at the loss of his sword, but soon even this thought faded from his mind to be replaced by the blank tension of battle-readiness, as vast and alert as the night. Slowly shifting his feet across the ground to find the best footing, he kept his eyes on the scrawny, voracious demons that had begun to slip into the clearing around him. Desert wolves!

Though they were named for the dunes of the desert, the wolves' territory lay chiefly among the rocky crags that rose high above the sands. Now it seemed to Guin as if every wolf in all of Nospherus had come to assail him. He could hear the sound of the spittle dripping the fangs in their slavering maws as they lusted after the rare treat of fresh flesh that stood unsubdued before them. Their foul breath was chokingly thick in the air.

Defiantly Guin roared. As if responding to a signal, the first wolf leapt for his throat!

Chapter Three

THE WOLF KING OF DOG'S HEAD MOUNTAIN

I

"Hrraarh!"

Guin's terrific battle cry scorched the air in the boulder-strewn clearing as the first of the attacking wolves arced toward him, its long fangs bared, its tongue a firebrand in the gloom.

The wolf's vicious howl mingled with Guin's cry. A moment later, the two opponents—beast and half-beast—collided in mid-air.

Nospherus was a trackless wilderness, regarded by every human society as an utter wasteland, the veritable end of the earth. The Kanan range stood at its far eastern edge, extending a ragged spur of ridges and foothills deep into the desert—a spur that included the tallest peak in all of the range, the peculiarly shaped Mount Pherus, known to the Sem as the Dog's Head. The rugged terrain here was distant indeed from domains of men, nor had anyone or anything ever attempted to bring even a vestige of order or civilization to its wildness.

Even the Sem avoided the land around the Dog's Head, preferring the lower lying valleys further to the west for their homes. The mountain was not a place for those who spoke with words, but for those who ran in packs and hunted in the night. It was the beasts' domain—or perhaps it belonged not to the beasts, but to some higher powers that kept the beasts there as a guard to protect the inviolate sanctity of their realm.

The rocky crags rose black and silent, while among them the stone-mimics and desert wolves moved with the howling winds through steep, pathless rock-fields. To face the mountain meant to face such monsters. It also meant to face thirst and exhaustion, and another, even greater hardship: an absolute, oppressive solitude that would have overwhelmed most travelers with the vastness of its harsh desolation. It was a path no man would choose unless driven by some terrible purpose, and yet one hero now faced it, alone, in the night.

Before that foolhardy, reckless traveler, the mountain now placed its first challenge.

The desert wolves were among the most legendary residents of the Nospherus highlands. As their name suggested, they had once lived in the desert, where they ran in ravening packs, sweeping across the sands like a violent white mirage. In those times, the wolves had been a constant threat to the territory of the Sem tribes and had pushed even the bigmouths and sandworms out of the central desert. In the ancient ruins of the east, carven reliefs could be seen that depicted in painstaking detail images of wolf-packs hundreds strong, their swift progress across the sands on soft-furred feet frozen in time by artisans long since dead. If the coloration of those murals could be trusted, the desert wolves of that time had been pure white from the whorls of thick fur on their heads to the tips of their long tails; their pale fur was the perfect camouflage against the white sands of their hunting grounds.

But the time when the desert wolves ruled the sands was long ago indeed, for it was the same ancient era when the Empire of Kanan still held sway in the desert and the mountains, and the Middle Country was but a wild jungle, overrun with hairy barbarians.

In the years since, the imperial city of Kanan had faded to a ruin buried in the sands, a legend lost somewhere among the Kanan Mountains. In that long lost time a great change of unknown origin had come to Nospherus, transforming everything to the east and north of the Dog's Head into a wasteland even bleaker than the desert, and nearly devoid of familiar forms of life. It was around this time that the wolves had abandoned their desert kingdom for the high crags, although none could say for certain when or why.

There was a legend about this time, which said that one night a corner of the sky had ripped open and death had fallen to the earth. According to this story the deathfall had spurred a great migration, driving all the creatures of the desert westward and further westward, transforming the region now known as the Marches into a teeming chaos of immigrant monstrosities. The fleeing beasts had run day in and day out, paying no heed to each other as they moved ever toward the west. Then, in the months that followed, the yidoh and other, stranger creatures had appeared to take their place in the empty wastes left behind.

While the truth of the legend might never be known, there could be no doubt that the yidoh and their kin had indeed taken over the low desert of Nospherus, while the wolves had moved into the rocky region around the Dog's Head and made it their home.

Over time, the white fur, which had helped to hide the wolves among the sands of Nospherus, had faded to a dark gray, and after many generations in the cold highlands, their pelts had become thick and bushy.

Two qualities of the desert wolves that had not changed were their vicious temperament and their pack-hunting instinct. It was these characteristics that made these wolves the most feared of all the dangers of Nospherus. Among the Sem that lived in the valleys nearest to the rocky regions where the dread canines prowled, the quickest way to achieve recognition as a great warrior for the likes of Ilateli of the Guro was to fight with a desert wolf and bring home its pelt.

Such were the beasts that Guin now faced in the night, high on the slopes of the Dog's Head with only a slender dagger between him and slavering death. He had lost his horse, most of his food, and his cherished war-sword, and now he seemed likely to lose his life, as a hundred pairs of gleaming eyes revealed where the mighty pack closed in on him, slinking between rock and crag, creeping over boulders and along the shadows of the ledges.

The first of the wolves to leap met a quick end as the point of Guin's dagger pierced its belly. The creature gave a last sorrowful death-cry as the leopard warrior dashed its bleeding bulk against a rock. Its demise provoked a frenzy as the other wolves immediately began to fight with gnashing fangs over the body of their comrade. Game was scarce in the Nospherus hills, and the pack was always in danger of starvation.

Yet while the closest wolves went for the carrion, others moved in on Guin, dancing across the rocks as they approached. Their threatening barks and howls of rage and the sound of their grinding jaws filled the air. Their musky stench thickened the night around the leopard-man and left a choking bitterness upon his tongue. Guin spat, and then with a quick movement he switched the dagger to his left hand. When the next wolf leapt, he was ready with a hardened fist to meet it.

The blow crushed the wolf's snout, sending it tumbling

back, snarling as it flew through the air. Guin did not spare the time to watch it go. Making sure that the boulder was still at his back, he slashed with the dagger in his left hand and kicked hard at a wolf to his right. Then like a dancer he jumped from foot to foot, striking and kicking at the howling beasts, his every limb a deadly weapon. The wolves came streaming in, like ants attacking a cornered mantis, pressing in against their lone foe. Guin fearlessly met their charge, aiming a kick at the gaping hot maw of one wolf, then plunging his dagger straight into the eye of the next even as he swung his right arm to punch it backwards.

There seemed to be no end to the dusky demons, but Guin paid no mind to their numbers, or their snapping jaws, or the smell of blood-matted fur that rose from the slick, hellish pool of gore that had formed at his feet. He paid these things no mind because he had no mind to pay. All human reason, knowledge, and emotion had evaporated from him. He was a beast, great and ferocious, a fearsome leopard, sleek pelt stained with blood, fangs dripping with the remnants of his fallen foes. His limbs knew no exhaustion or weakness. The limitless vitality and destructive will of nature itself now filled him, and he became king-like in his mighty rage, stomping and tossing and cutting down these footsoldiers of the enemy.

This was not the Guin that Rinda and Remus had witnessed single-handedly dispatching a squad of black knights near the

Roodspring. This was something far greater and wilder, an avatar of destruction and death, hardly recognizable as the twins' stalwart guardian. His body from the neck down may have looked like a man's, but this blood-soaked creature that howled and ripped at the throats of its enemies was far from human. And no human, not even one trained for years and hardened in battle, a warrior among warriors, could have held out half as long against half as many wolves as did Guin.

He was a leopard, a massive, bloodthirsty cat that toyed with its foes. His joy in the fight shone in his fiery red eyes, his blood-drenched fangs, and the agile and powerful grace of his movements. He was one and the same with the wolves that clustered around him, eager to rend his flesh and drink his blood. The wolves knew it. This was no tragic battle between man and animal. This was a war between beasts, following the sacred rules of such conflicts; blind to all niceties of fairness or honor, lacking any room for mercy or compassion, it was a struggle of tooth and claw.

The largest wolf of the pack vaulted into the air, and when Guin beat it back there was a sharp snap. His dagger had broken in half. Howling, Guin tossed the blade from his hand, sticky with blood.

Then the leopard-man whirled, still keeping the rock to his back, and dodged away from another wolf, grabbing the fiend by

its tail as it soared by. Then, holding the thick tail like the haft of a club, he swung the hapless creature in a great arc to the left and right, knocking several of its packmates back into the darkness.

A new cry of rage burst from Guin's lips, for while he was swinging the wolf, another had crept up onto the rock behind him and then jumped down to land on his back, where it sank its long fangs into his shoulder. Guin howled once more, then threw the wolf he was carrying into the path of the others in front of him and grabbed onto the beast at his back with both hands, trying to pry open the thing's jaws. His every muscle tensed as he moved his left hand to the wolf's throat and lifted sharply upward.

There was an unsettling popping sound, and the strength went out of the creature's jaws. Its head hanging limply from its twisted neck, the wolf dropped off Guin's back and landed with a thud on the ground.

Yet by this time, another wolf had seen its opening and leapt down from atop the rock. Guin ducked and grabbed its gray body as it sailed over him, slamming it into a jagged projection of stone. His eyes gleamed red and he surveyed the clearing with the cold stare of a hunter.

The smell of blood on the wind and the howls and death rattles of the wolves had announced the terrible fray far across the rocks and crags. Though Guin had killed or otherwise disabled no small number of wolves, there seemed to be no fewer of the beasts around him than before, their eyes gleaming and their heads low, ready to lunge in for the kill. They were like the ghouls of the Marches, constantly multiplying, a new foe springing up to replace each one he cut down. Their hundred pairs of eyes were like stars in hell, glowing with a dark fire.

The hair stood on the back of Guin's neck, and a low rattling growl of warning sounded in his throat. He looked around, hesitating in a momentary lull in the struggle. It was not reason, but his animal instincts that gave him pause.

Continue to fight and you will lose.

Civilized man had morals, logic, chivalry, the impulses of temperament, and the urgings of honor. But a true beast was encumbered by none of these things; it knew only the merciless contest and a blind, basic instinct for self-preservation. Now Guin's instinct had spoken to him, and he would heed it.

For a moment the leopard-man's fanged mouth hung open as he uttered a last threatening growl at those fiery eyes. But he was no longer interested in winning this battle. Dodging the wolves that leapt for him, he turned suddenly and shot like a bolt of lightning up the rock face he had stood against, then began to bound away, leaping from boulder to boulder like the winged taulos, making his escape.

A great cry rose up from the darkness—the wolves had tasted

blood, and they did not want to give up their prey. Swiftly the pack gave chase. Wolves vaulted to the tops of boulders and wound their way between the rocks. Their quarry did not stop to look back.

The lead wolf sprang from a boulder-top towards Guin's retreating back, aiming its fangs for the base of his leopard skull, but it was as if the giant warrior had eyes in the back of his head. With uncanny accuracy, Guin sensed the beast's trajectory, and just before it reached him ducked and leapt aside and was off to the next boulder, leaving the wolf to snap its jaws upon the empty dark.

Guin's chest rose and fell like a massive pair of bellows, sending air into his lungs, and he moved with an unconsciously surefooted grace across the jagged, pointed rocks. From his feline muzzle to his leather waistband, Guin was slick with wolf blood and grimed with clots of hair and bits of flesh. He could hear the baying of hundreds more of the beasts in pursuit, running across the rocks behind him and along the ground beneath his feet. They were relentless hunters, seemingly determined to avenge the deaths the leopard-man had brought them.

In many ways, Guin's situation now was even worse than when he had faced the pack in the clearing, moments before. His path was dark and unfamiliar, and despite their rough appearance, the boulders were deceptively smooth and slippery, and his boots

were soaked in wolf blood. One false step on the uneven stone—
one slip of his gore-slick feet—and he would fall upon the jagged
rocks that stuck up like knives between the larger boulders that
formed his elevated path. Even if the fall did not kill him, it would
only be a matter of moments before the pack caught up to him
and tore his wounded body into bloody chunks.

Yet he never hesitated. Without stopping once to check his
footing he ran on with incredible speed, like a laurelled runner
on a track he had known since birth. Not once did his pace fal-
ter, and whenever a gap or chasm yawned before him he jumped
fearlessly through the night air. He was beautiful, like a titanic
cheetah, an athlete of mythical splendor.

He ran, and the wolves ran. It was a contest between the
killers and the one who would be killed, the hunters and the
hunted, and yet they looked like a great king leading his army on
a charge, or a heroic saint and his frenzied flock, preserving a
heterodox harmony as they chased the wind.

So similar did they appear, the massive leopard-headed
beast-god and the starving wolves of the crags, that it seemed as
if there were some mystic connection between them. The sound
of Guin's breathing mingled with the panting of the wolves, and
the sound of their footfalls echoed his as they fell behind, then
drew closer, only to fall behind once again.

Eventually the boulders began to grow scarcer on the slope

ahead. Guin's path had led him straight up the mountainside;
now his breath formed a white mist against the night sky. The
moon goddess Aeris seemed to pace restlessly across the heavens
above him, as though she, too, was a participant in the life-and-
death chase below.

Mingled with his own heavy breathing, Guin could hear the
howling of the wolves as they closed the distance behind him.
He searched for some feature of the terrain that might aid him
in losing the wolves for good—a narrow ravine, a valley blocked
by boulders, a fallen log—anything but this endless scree field.
A plan was beginning to form in his mind, but he needed to
find an advantage in the landscape, and it seemed that there was
nothing ahead but rocks and the mountain sloping ever upwards. The boulder-field came to a gradual end, and ahead of
him the mountain's face was black and unbroken. He was
nearing the summit.

This was not the salvation Guin had hoped for. Here the
big rocks were fewer, and there were neither shrubs nor any
other cover to conceal him. Atop the boulders, Guin's agility
had given him the advantage, and he had gained a good lead on
the wolves; out here in the open their foot speed, which had
once made them so feared among the dunes of the desert, would
surely give them the edge.

To circle back would have been impossible, and it seemed

that there was little chance of escape higher up on the peak. His dagger had snapped sometime during the fighting. At this point, with an apparent dead end ahead and all weapons broken or lost, most warriors, even great heroes, would have looked to the heavens and cast their arms up in despair, calling out to their guardian spirits in some hope that divine intervention would save them where all their luck and skill had failed. But Guin's shining red eyes were expressionless pools, void of emotion; he seemed to have descended into a trance beneath his rigid mask.

Some essential quality, something vital that makes a man a part of humanity, had disappeared from Guin's eyes. He was a warrior still, but at some point he had become all animal. Perhaps it was the fear of death, that all-too-human fear of the unknown that lurked beyond the last breath, that was missing. In its place was an all-powerful instinct for self-preservation that enabled him to act without hindrance from the clouding veil of emotion. Guin knew no despair—in his current state, the concept would not have made sense to him. Trapped on the mountainside, the leopard-headed warrior showed no cowardice; he simply charged confidently toward the peak as though he expected a life-rope to be dangling down from the stars, waiting to carry him away.

His feet thudded on the soft ground. The last of the sharp rocks that might have slowed the passage of the wolves were behind him. As soon as he had left the last rock he sprinted up the slope, never slowing down, his endurance unflagging. His leather cape flowed out behind him, its hem tattered and torn by the sharp rocks and sharper fangs of the wolves. His chest heaving, Guin ran.

The wolves had the clear advantage. Their four muscular legs were well adapted to running on smooth terrain. Rapidly they ate up the distance Guin had gained in the boulder-field, and soon they were running around him in a pack, like hounds running alongside a huntsman. One of them picked up speed and sprang into the air, followed quickly by ten others in a fierce wave, launching themselves at Guin's shoulders, his legs, his chest, and his arms like carnivorous fish swarming on a hapless steer.

Guin howled. If they dragged him down here, he was finished. With flailing fists he beat them off; still the creatures multiplied, coming in wave after wave. Should he slip, he knew that in an instant he would be buried underneath a mountain of the fur-covered demons. His legs tensed. There was no time left to find a good position from which to ward off the wolves coming at him from all sides, and yet he could run no further. Muscles tightened like sinewy ropes stretching across his body, he braced himself to throw off the next attack.

Two more wolves lunged for his throat, and with lightning reflexes he grabbed them both. Then dexterously he tucked one under each arm and, squeezing them to his sides with tremendous strength, broke both their necks. The air was filled with their whines of pain and then the popping of their bones, punctuated by the howls of the surrounding wolves. This was a battle unlike any that ordinary men could ever know. The leopard king faced the thronging, bloodthirsty canine horde, neither side seeking the other's pity, neither side relying on words to parley or threaten. It was a brutal fight without emotion, mercy, restraint, or any hope of reconciliation.

Guin was in dire straits, yet he made neither prayer nor sign, no last appeal to the heavens for aid. The only thing that could put out the fire that burned in his eyes was a lethal, physical blow to the throat or heart, and he knew that he need fear nothing more or less than this. He knew no despair, and yet he clung to no mad hope that he might survive. Like a machine, an apparatus of death, blind to all else, he saw only the battle.

Yet it seemed that even Guin had reached his limits at last. Though he fought tirelessly, his breathing had grown more strenuous as he fended off the endless stream of wolves, always on the attack, each rushing to fill the space where a pack-mate had fallen, dodging the carcasses with broken necks that he threw at them.

Now his own blood streamed from his shoulders, legs, and thighs, mixing with the blood from the wolves that soaked him.

He was surrounded, and try though he might he could not dodge them all. Every other bite got past his defenses and struck at his exposed flesh. He howled in pain, a roar of rage that burst from deep within, and tossed another wolf corpse, its neck dangling, at the pack; still the beasts came on. One slavering shadow ducked low and sped closer, dodging under Guin's guard, and leapt up to lock its teeth around his throat.

Guin grabbed the beast's bloody maw with both hands, trying to pry it off, leaving his back undefended for an instant. Almost immediately, his body shook with a blow from behind, and a stab of pain burned like a firebrand into his spine. The largest wolf yet had pounced onto his back, sinking its teeth into his shoulder blade. Guin struggled to remain standing, but the dragging weight from both directions was too much for him, and he fell to one knee.

The wolves had been waiting for just this opportunity. In a flurry of motion they came at him from all sides, mouths frothing with anticipation. His eyes were like plates of glass, showing no pain, no despair, merely reflecting the thronging pack that now descended upon him like angels of death.

His body fought on, writhing and striking at the wolves, knocking aside their fangs.

And then Guin sensed a presence beyond the snarling wolves. *He* had arrived.

—— 2 ——

At first, neither Guin nor the wolves understood what had taken place. As the leopard-headed warrior fell to his back with the frenzied canines roaring over him, he heard a peculiar wolf-cry—a sorrowful keening that cut through the baying of the pack. In moments the howls around him became screams of pain, and then soft, piteous whines.

Pinned under gray furred bodies Guin had no idea what was going on, but from the sound it seemed as if someone or something was quickly and violently dispatching the wolves. After a few moments the jaws of the big wolf that had seized his neck reluctantly loosened, and the fangs of its pack-mate withdrew from the taut muscles of the leopard-man's shoulder. Guin was free.

Yet the respite from attack brought him little pleasure, for now the pain and exhaustion that he had not felt in the rush of the fight hit him all at once. His head throbbed as if it were crushed in a vice and his strength seemed to seep from the bleeding fang marks that covered his body. With his mind reeling he lay on the cold ground.

Dimly, then, he realized that the night had become utterly quiet, save for the occasional soft panting that told him the wolves were still there. What had happened? Guin tried to sit up. His throat, his back, and his arms and legs ached as though all the muscles in his body were split and fraying. A fiery pain burned along the pathways of his nerves, and he slumped back down to the ground. But his curiosity and a suspicion that he was not yet safe overcame the crippling pain. Gritting his teeth and holding back a whimper he pushed himself up again, then rose to his feet...

And then Guin saw him.

He drew in a sharp breath. Whatever it was he had thought might have saved him from the wolf pack's clutching jaws, it was not this. Guin's bright eyes widened with surprise and shone with doubt at the truth of what they witnessed. At that moment, a bit of the humanity that had gone dormant while the leopard-headed warrior raged in battle rose again in his mind like a diver poking his head through the surface of the sea after a long foray into its depths.

"This is a surprise," Guin muttered, his voice hesitant and his tongue thick in his mouth, as though he had forgotten speech for long ages and was just now remembering the shape of words.

"*You* saved me? *You?*"

The moon shone brightly as the goddess Aeris glided out from behind a cloud where she had taken refuge, casting her pale light on the cursed land once again. Guin's battle with the wolves had seemed to last an eternity, but in truth it had only been a half-*twist* since he first faced them in the clearing among the boulders. In that time, the moon had slid ever so slightly toward the horizon, while Jarn's Eye shone from its perch due east above the mountain summit.

In the ghostly light that poured from the heavens, Guin could see his savior clearly with his night-worthy animal eyes. It was a wolf, a great demon of the crags, so massive as to make even the largest wolf he had seen up until then seem no more than a newborn cub. It was not only the creature's size that provoked Guin's amazement but also the shining silver-white radiance of the pelt—as pale and gleaming as the snows of Ashgarn—that covered its giant frame from the tightly curled fur on its head to the tip of its bushy tail.

"*You* saved me?" repeated Guin. Somehow, he knew that the wolf could understand his words, though he could not have said whether it heard them as men do or somehow sensed their meaning from the waves of startled emotion. The wolf moved closer, snarling a low, clear warning to one of the smaller wolves which still panted in anticipation of a kill.

He stood above Guin on the tip of a broad outcrop that thrust up from the ground, peering over its edge like a king sitting on a high throne. His size and the power of his presence seemed to fill the sky. This was, without a doubt, the lord of the Dog's Head—and it was obvious that he knew it. His eyes shone with a piercing silver light from under his white brow, and his slow, graceful movements and the way those silver orbs fixed upon Guin, as though gauging his worth, made clear the great wolf's utter confidence and authority.

Guin was in the court of the Wolf King of Dog's Head Mountain.

Guin's amber eyes met the pale eyes of the Wolf King and the air crackled between them. The Wolf King returned the leopard warrior's gaze without blinking, as though he was weighing whether or not Guin's value was such as warranted rescuing. The great beast's eyes were filled with the immeasurable sagacity of a creature that had lived for years beyond count, sharpened by an almost human-like intellect that now probed and considered the mighty interloper who had appeared in his ancient realm.

The ashen-gray wolves around him stood motionless, awaiting their king's decision. Guin, too, stood perfectly still. The moon slid behind another cloud, then reemerged, playing its mythic light across the mountainside; a tense, stifling silence pervaded the scene. Then at last the Wolf King slowly tilted his head to one side and howled a low, commanding howl that, it seemed to Guin, bore the tone of a command.

As one, the wolves of the Dog's Head silently turned and began to slink away. Some among the pack whined in their throats, reluctant to give up the feast they thought was theirs, but they were silenced with a glare from their king. Curling their tails beneath them they trotted quickly out of sight, heading back towards the boulder-field below. In a few moments, all the desert wolves that had surrounded Guin were gone.

When the last few stragglers had disappeared, casting regretful backward looks as they went, Guin felt the night suddenly grow cool around him. Alone he stood, facing the Wolf King, who had grown as still as the stone beneath him.

He could sense no enmity coming from the Wolf King's eyes. Rather, when the great wolf turned his eyes back to Guin after checking to see that all of his subjects had indeed gone back down the slope, they had a look of familiarity, a sparkle that seemed to say: *I know you well, leopard-man.*

The blood that flowed from Guin's wounds was beginning to dry. His entire body ached and stung with pain, and his arms and legs were impossibly heavy with exhaustion; yet he stood, immobile as a statue, waiting to discover what the great creature would do. Finally the Wolf King padded slowly down the rock to-

wards Guin with soft, even steps, as though to show he meant
no harm. With each step, his white fur rippled and swayed; he
was like a spirit come from the wild eternal snows of the highest
Ashgarn peaks. Soaked in moonlight, the silver streaks in his fur
gleamed like frost. Approaching the still motionless Guin, the
Wolf King stretched out his neck and brought his snout close to
Guin's unclenched fist. Then, without a sound, he respectfully
licked the leopard-headed warrior's hand.

When the rough, cold tongue touched the leopard-man's
fingers it sent a shiver like a bolt of lightning through his body.
He was seized by a sudden uncontrollable trembling that he did
not understand, and he stared at the Wolf King with a look of
amazement, feeling as if…as if he was gazing upon his own destiny. Guin had a sudden sense that this meeting had been in-
evitable, as though Jarn's hands had woven every step of his path
up the mountain. And then it struck the leopard warrior that the
Wolf King had expected this encounter all along, that he had
seen the pattern and had come down from his throne to guide
Guin to this place.

Guin stared silently at the Wolf King. Something remarkable was happening inside the battle-scarred warrior. From the
damp flat of his hand where the wolf's coarse tongue had touched
it, some divine, untamed spirit of the wilds was flowing into his
body, refilling the wellspring of vitality deep within him until it

overflowed. Faster than he could believe, the terrible exhaustion that had overcome him, the pain of his wounds, and even the thirst that clutched at his throat all lifted and disappeared.

In their place, a limitless, primal life-force now surged through his body, flowing under his skin, along his pulsing veins, and into his mighty limbs. Slowly Guin lifted his hand and placed it on the steely whorled fur atop the wolf's giant head. As though he was observing the steps of some timeless ritual, the ancient beast stood perfectly still, letting Guin's hand rest upon him for a while. Then he slowly withdrew and, after licking the leopard-man's fingers one final time, fixed him with a gaze full of inscrutable meaning. Then he turned and began silently to pad away.

Impulsively, Guin raised a hand and stepped out to follow the beast, but the wolf stopped a short distance away and shot him a look that said, *Do not follow*, and began to run, his silver-white form quickly disappearing into the night.

Guin felt a sudden certainty that the Wolf King meant for him to remain there and await his savior's return. He looked around, and after satisfying himself that there was nothing of danger waiting for him in the shadows, he sat upon the night-chilled ground. Though he should have been tired and horribly weakened, he felt strangely elated, and as fresh as though he had just awoken from a long and restful sleep. He stretched out till he was comfortable, yet remained watchful of danger, and thought about the creature he had just encountered.

There was a power and majesty in the Wolf King's presence that bespoke a spirit greater than that of any mere beast, perhaps greater than that of any mortal creature of the world. It was something profound and divine. Had he transformed before Guin's eyes into an old man with long white whiskers and announced himself as an avatar of the desert land, forced to take the guise of a wolf for some reason, Guin would not have been surprised; there had been something about the great creature's form, something deep within his eyes, that was wild beyond words. It was an essence that expressed all that was noble in animal nature.

Guin reflected on the Wolf King's white fur. He knew of tales (though for the life of him, he could not remember who had told them, or when) according to which, long ago, when the desert wolves ruled the desert, their pelts had been prized for their pure, snow-white beauty. It was only after they had been driven into the mountains that they had become ashen-hued, resembling nothing so much as evil phantoms, haunting the crags high above the sands. Yet the tales told that even now, once in a great while, a throwback to the wolves' desert-dwelling days would be born: a pup with pure white fur. When these pups grew larger, they were hunted by the Sem; in civilized countries, their pelts would fetch almost ten times their weight in gold.

Perhaps this Wolf King is one of those throwbacks, thought Guin. Yet the great wolf was so large in comparison to the rest of the Nospherus pack, he thought it more likely that the creature had come from a different stock altogether. Or could the ancient beast be the last of the wolves that had roamed the desert sand—a survivor from their distant past? Guin let out a laugh and discarded this idea. Many years indeed had come and gone since the desert wolves had truly lived among the dunes.

There was a soft sound away across the slope. Guin sprang to his feet, then relaxed and let the alert tension leave his muscles. The Wolf King had returned. The great white beast approached the leopard-man slowly, his head down as if to apologize for taking so long. He was carrying something in his jaws. Placing it at Guin's feet, he nodded his head and drew back, like a vassal giving an offering to his holy lord. Then, lowering his ghostly form silently to the ground, he laid his head on his two front paws and regarded Guin with a steady stare. His gaze seemed more friendly and companionable than before.

Guin picked up the Wolf King's offering. It was a plump balto bird with iridescent wings, freshly killed and still warm. Guin looked at the Wolf King, who was waiting hesitantly, as if to see whether the offering met Guin's taste. Guin nodded and brought it to his mouth without hesitation.

The sweet, fresh blood ran down his throat and quenched his thirst. Then with sharp fangs he ripped into the fat bird as though he was a beast born. He devoured it eagerly, driven by a wild hunger that he had forgotten about until this moment. His jaw flexed, crunching bone and feather with a snapping sound.

The Wolf King looked on, seeming satisfied by this performance. Guin, looking up for a moment from his engrossing feast, noticed the creature's stare, and he tore a wing off the bird and offered it to the wolf. The wolf refused, pushing it back with his nose, but when Guin insisted, he acquiesced, a servant graciously accepting gifts from his master, and began to eat.

It did not take long for Guin to consume the whole juicy bird. This wild meal was the most delicious, most satisfying feast he could remember. It was like nectar from the gods; he felt as though he was receiving life itself through his jaws, pure and raw and satisfying. He was lapping up the blood from his hands and the edge of his mouth with a long rasping tongue, when the sheer naturalness of what he was doing occurred to him.

Am I truly a beast? Drinking the blood, crushing the bones of this balto, I find it more delicious than any meal that could be prepared by the culinarists of the civilized lands. A beast-man...this is all I am. What would Rinda, little queen of Parros, think if she saw me here, sitting with a wolf, eating with bloody mouth and tongue?

She'd probably scream and faint, Guin admitted to himself. Inevitably his thoughts were drawn to the question that had plagued him since he awoke in the Roodwood with all memory gone. Who was he? How had he become like this? This time, however, the doubt did not bother him as much. He was full, and he was tired. By his side, the Wolf King, who had been busily engaged in grooming himself, licking his paws and chest, now stopped and suggested by pantomime that Guin go to sleep, laying his head down on his forelegs and closing his eyes.

"You're a clever one, aren't you?" remarked the leopard-man, laughing aloud. "But I suppose I should take your advice. After all, it seems quite clear someone's sent you to aid me. I'm through with wondering at the strangeness that befalls me. It's against my nature, and besides, what will come will come. Wolf King, I trust you, and I'll assume that whoever sent you did so with my best interests in mind. At the very least, that bird you brought me was the most delicious thing I've ever eaten, and surely that is a good sign. It's a shame you cannot speak! For if you could, I imagine you could tell me a great deal—about my being, my true nature, my destiny—all the things I so dearly want to know!"

Guin rambled on freely as though he were talking to an old friend. The Wolf King listened intently, his eyes open and ears perked, as if he was trying to concentrate and understand what

Guin said. But whether he understood or not, his clever animal eyes revealed nothing. At last he laid down his head and closed his eyes again, signaling once more that Guin should sleep. Guin laughed and nodded, then stretched his arms and legs, lay supine and shut his eyes.

Night was chilly on the Dog's Head, but the leopard-man's leather cloak protected him well, and his trained body was hardened enough to allow him to sleep almost anywhere without discomfort. It was not long before his spirit was roaming through the mountains of Dream.

For a while, the Wolf King stayed perfectly still, as though afraid of waking the warrior from his slumber. At long last, he lifted his head and looked over at his companion.

Guin seemed to be deep asleep. Reassured, the Wolf King rose slowly to his feet. Stretching and shaking the dirt from his belly, he slunk over to Guin and looked at his still face. Then, blinking his startlingly deep and thoughtful eyes, he gently licked Guin's forehead, careful not to wake him.

The Wolf King seemed filled with respect and even fear, like an aged noble doing homage to his beloved emperor; he resembled, too, some tribal elder, a sage, gently acknowledging his successor, still young, with many things to learn. In a way that was far deeper than physical form, the two resembled each other—the giant silver-white wolf, king of Dog's Head Mountain, and the mighty leopard-headed warrior sleeping at his feet. Powerful, self-reliant spirits, they could easily have been kinsmen from the same tribe, even brothers, so close did they seem.

The look they shared was that of one who had been chosen by something greater than himself to bear a burden of destiny so heavy that an ordinary mortal would stagger under its weight; one who had been blessed with strength and endurance of the spirit, yet who had to fight a terrible battle with no hope of aid or salvation. Very few were they who lived such a life, and they were truly alone, though their victories made the hearts of other men soar high. Such as these were known as heroes.

Guin's body twitched and then shuddered as a dream disturbed his sleep. The Wolf King looked on worriedly for a short while; then, seeing that the warrior had fallen back into a calmer slumber, the great canine turned and departed silently across the rocks, headed out on some new task. His white form shone like a phantom against the dark crags and the starry sky.

The night was deep, but not as dark as it had been a few moments before. Dawn was approaching. The stars wheeled on their set courses, and the pale Aeris sped away to the western horizon, as though seeking to escape the advances of her fiery morning suitor, Ruah Sungod. A glow of indigo crept across the heavens as Ruah cast a white portent of his glorious birth over the eastern horizon, and the great spirit of the sky, Ayi, began rolling up his star-studded curtain to greet the day.

Morning had come again to Nospherus. It was the beginning of the second of the four days in which Guin had promised the combined armies of the Sem that he would return with rein-forcements. It was also the morning that the Lady Amnelis planned to lead her mighty host on a raid to exterminate the Sem once and for all.

Guin slept. No heartless beast, stone-mimic, stonesnake, or leech-kin came to harass him. It was as though a mystic pen-tagram had been laid in the soil around him, forming a barrier against anything that might disturb his slumber.

The first ray of sun came over the Dog's Head as though blazing Ruah had poked a giant arm through the curtain of the night. The Wolf King appeared on an outcropping, again car-rying something in his mouth. It was a rock-lizard—as juicy as a balto bird, and tasting much the same. Laying it near Guin, he once more slipped away in silence. When he next returned, he was carrying a fragrant sweet cactus in his mouth. He had pre-pared a fine breakfast for the sleeping warrior.

Setting the cactus down by the rock-lizard, the Wolf King took up a position at Guin's head, standing like a protective watch-hound. By now Ruah's fiery disk had risen high enough to cast the first true light of morning on the mountain rocks. Bathed in that light, the silvery-white wolf shone more brilliantly than the glaciers of Ashgarn, so bright that any lesser eyes that looked upon him would have been dazzled.

It was an exhilaratingly beautiful scene, like something out of a fable or legend of old: the king of Dog's Head Mountain, awaiting the leopard-hero's rise, standing perfectly still and shining like a morning star on the mountaintop.

—— 3 ——

Morning had come to Nospherus, and the harsh light of the desert sun burnished the jagged peaks of the mountains.

Guin woke to the sensation of a cold, wet nose thrust hesitantly at his hands. His eyes opened with a start and he jumped to his feet to see the Wolf King standing beside him, his fur shining white like high-mountain snow in the glow of morning. The great wolf stared at him with large, silver eyes.

"I was dreaming." Guin spoke to the beast with casual familiarity, as though he had been living here on the Dog's Head, running with the wolf pack, for many years. "I dreamt I was a king. There was a shining crown upon my head, and holy priests draped the purple vestments of royalty on my shoulders in the high temple of Janos. And the people—there were great and joyous crowds, and they were calling for me, calling my name.

"I remember seeing the Dawn Star. I clasped it in my hand, and when it slipped free and sought to escape I chased after it, against the wishes of my people who would have me stay. I threw down my crown and my scepter and my robes, until I was free of all tokens, a simple warrior once more.

"I remember walking on a long, red road, though I know not where it led. Then suddenly a strange wizened fellow appeared before me. He had one eye in the middle of his forehead, long flowing whiskers, and the body of a goat from the waist down. He wore a triangular cloth upon his head, and in his hand he bore a gnarled, crooked staff.

"Even as I looked upon him his single eye flared red. He struck me with the staff, yelling, 'Fool! Go back! Take back the throne of the dragon...'"

Guin scratched his head, puzzled. "I'm sure the old goatman was Jarn Fateweaver. But what could it mean—the message, and the dream?"

The wolf gave no answer; instead he silently nuzzled Guin's arm with his nose, drawing the warrior's attention to the breakfast he had brought for him. Guin smiled and patted the great wolf on his head. Then he busied himself peeling off the sand lizard's rough skin. Then, breaking the sweet cactus in two, he began to eat. Despite his incredible adventures of the day before, Guin had rested well, and his limbs felt full of energy. All his fatigue had been wiped away.

The Wolf King stood quietly watching the ravenous warrior

devour the wild morsels that made up his breakfast. Occasion-
ally Guin glanced up to marvel at the silvery-white animal before
him that seemed to combine the magnificence of a wild beast
with an awareness that was somehow human—and yet possessed
an aura of power far greater than those of such mortal creatures.

When the leopard-man had finished eating, the Wolf King
gazed deliberately into his face as if to ask him if he was satisfied. Then, nuzzling Guin once more with his nose, he turned
and began to trot away. Guin sat, watching him go, but when
the wolf saw that he was not moving, the great animal promptly
returned and with an air of irritation put his jaws on Guin's
hand and tugged, taking care not to bite too hard. Then he trotted away again in the same direction—towards the peak of Dog's
Head Mountain—his white tail swaying back and forth behind
him as he went.

"First you're my savior, now you're my guide. When will the
wonders cease?" Guin asked, rising to follow the retreating wolf.
"Maybe old man Jarn sent you? I wonder if you know that I have
just two and half days to find the Lagon and bring them back to
the Sem? But then, if you're going to show me the right path to
follow, you may well convince me that you're not sent by Jarn,
but are Jarn himself, in one of his hundred forms. Come to
think of it, the old man's whiskers in my dream this morning
were white like yours."

Jarn or no, you and the cyclone that brought me here were both heaven-sent. Someone up there is telling me to do something, here on the slopes of the Dog's Head, that much is clear.

Guin shook his head. He was forgetting where he was: Nospherus, a land forsaken by the gods. Sandstorms, even cyclones like the one the day before, were not all that uncommon, though certainly most were smaller than the roving cataclysm that had carried him into the mountains. It might just have been a coincidence that the cyclone had been moving in the direction he wished to go, mere chance that it had picked him up and taken him along his path. It may also have been presumptuous of him to assume that the Wolf King had been sent on some divine mission, for that matter. Everything that had happened in the last two days could be no more than the whim of fortune. And the Wolf King's strange behavior—well, beasts such as he that had grown to an incredible age were known for their wisdom and strange powers of perception. He could be acting entirely on his own, for purposes known only to him.

There was no need, thought Guin, to be overly superstitious about the events of the past day, uncanny though they seemed. *It's the future I need to think about.* He followed the Wolf King, while his eyes ceaselessly darted across the slopes and rocky hollows, looking out for danger.

After a short distance the Wolf King stopped and peered

back to make sure that Guin was following. Seeing that the leop-ard-headed warrior was indeed keeping pace a ways behind him, he turned back around and set off more quickly than before, glancing back after every five or six motad to make sure that Guin still followed. Though Guin now found himself walking quite fast, he knew that the wolf was going much slower than he could have, for Guin's benefit.

The course they took went steadily uphill, toward the moun-tain's peak. They seemed to be headed for the narrow pass that crossed directly over the head of the dog, weaving between the high crags that jutted out on either side to form the ears. Guin had come a considerable way up the mountainside while fleeing from the wolf pack the night before. Still, the winding path they now took up the last stretch below the summit was surprisingly long and steep. The two ears appeared almost close enough to touch, yet no matter how long they walked they never seemed to reach the top.

The unlikely companions continued up the mountain in silence. Guin was drawing on his animal endurance now, never stopping as a man might to wipe the sweat from his brow nor pausing to catch his breath. When a boulder-fall blocked his path, he swiftly climbed up and over it. When the path changed to a ledge along a cliff-face, he carefully sidestepped along it, never falling far behind his swift-footed guide.

The scenery was not the kind that made for a pleasurable climb. The Dog's Head was a rocky, Nospherus peak, and though it was nominally part of the Kanan range, it jutted out alone into the desert, far from the main spine of the mountains. Although it was less tall than many of the lofty Ashgarns to the north, it had no rival in the parched desert nearby, and it could bee seen clearly from a great distance across the dunes.

The mountain looked like nothing so much as a mythic creature, a huge and sharp-faced dog that had sat so long in the stony sand that at last it had changed to rock itself. Though wolves lived in its skirts, and other desert creatures roamed its lower rifts and gullies, there was no green copse of trees to adorn its rugged slopes. In fact, nothing at all grew upon the higher ridges aside from the stone-mimics and a dry, gray lichen. Lower down, where Guin had found himself deposited by the sandstorm, there were thickets of sparse, thorny shrubs and cacti, but above them the mountain was as barren as the sands of the desert floor.

It was a difficult and increasingly tedious climb. The rock surface where the boulders had tumbled and split was the same ashen gray as that of the wolves, and its harsh contours gave no welcome to any grass or flower that might have hoped to catch in a cranny and grow. Once or twice the leopard-man glimpsed gray rock lizards scuttling across the stone; these along with the

slender rocksnakes and scurrying alpine insects were the pri-
mary food source of the desert wolves that made these heights
their home. Guin wondered where all the wolves that had assailed him the night before had now gone. Not a single one
crossed the path of the Wolf King and the strange interloper he
now led toward the summit.

The sun had already risen quite high in the eastern sky.
There was no obstruction of tree or cloud in the Nospherus
highlands to block its rays, and the difference between the chilly
nights and the blazing days was dramatic—and harshest of all here
up the Dog's Head. The cycle of fiery sun and frozen night had
given the rocks a hard sheen and kept even the hardiest of mosses
from gaining purchase on the dry crags.

Guin walked, half in a dream, along the monotonous ashen-
gray path. The glare off the rocks gradually put him in a sort of
trance, and his mind wandered through the bizarre landscape
that surrounded him. *Up here is the true no-man's land*, he
thought. *There are many mysteries in the world, half of which
man may never see or understand in this age. In Nospherus
alone there are numberless places where no man has ever tread,
gullies and crannies teeming with strangeness.* Guin felt suddenly that he was in the presence of some unearthly will, as invisible and yet as real as the dry wind upon his face. It was almost
as if the land had a fierce awareness of its own.

In a sense, the vast desert and rocky hills of Nospherus that stretched from the Kes River seemingly to the very edge of the world formed a single living entity, and the yidoh and bigeaters that dwelt in the wild land and the sandstorms that scoured its surface were nothing more than parasites upon it. This, then— the malevolent life-force of the land itself—was the source of the unnatural aura that hung in the air, indefinable but nonetheless distinctly present for Guin, the twins, and every soldier in the Mongauli expeditionary force. Each of these travelers in Nospherus had a sense that there was always something there, watching them, but look though they might, all they could ever see was sand and rock and sky.

Still, the reality of the place had a way of sinking in. Something about Nospherus was wrong, something more than its strange tangled chain of life, its monstrous flora and fauna, though these were peculiar enough. There was something in the land itself that was twisted. Those who crossed the Kes might not understand it, but they could feel it in their very blood.

Guin knew that it had not always been this way. He knew it the same way he knew the words of the Sem tongue and the history of the realms of the Middle Country. He could not remember learning it; the information was simply there. Nospherus had not always been the cursed home of Doal-spawned monstrosities and wildling tribes, Guin thought to himself now. He paused, gazing out across the ravaged land. The Wolf King shot him a questioning look and came back to him, brushing alongside his leg.

This is where the great Empire of Kanan, built by the Sun King, Rallah, once laid its long roads. All Nospherus was its glorious domain, a vast empire thriving between sand and rock. The Kananites used the desert and the mountains as natural defenses; they rode in boats that could sail the sands, and great waterworks carried their water from the high mountains so that even in the midst of the desert there was never thirst or drought. The glory of Kanan was greater than that of any kingdom in the Middle Country today...

Then Guin recalled the story told in Alzandross's *History*, of how a strange disaster had befallen the Empire of Kanan, a punishment sent down from the heavens that turned the majestic palaces and wide boulevards into dust overnight. Since then the domain of Kanan had been deserted and had lain unclaimed by any lord to the present day.

What happened to Nospherus? What could have destroyed such a mighty empire, and left nothing alive on the sands it once ruled but worms and foul yidoh? What could have taken the good-hearted people of Kanan, whose stories are sung in the tales of old, and left in their place only barbarous wildlings?

It was, to Guin, an utter mystery. Had he known the real

reason that the Mongauli court had taken a sudden interest in Nospherus, the terrible secret that had spurred their daring incursion into the desert—the tale that Cal Moru, spellcaster of Kitai, had told of the valley of Gur Nuu that lay deep in the desert's interior—he might have suspected that the valley and the strange stone it held had played a role in the transformation of Nospherus. But he knew none of this, least of all how the Golden Scorpion Palace now hoped to find in that valley a new and lethal weapon that would aid them in their conquest of the known world.

Yet with his uncanny intuition Guin sensed that there was something hidden in this land that would bring a great change to the currents of history in the world beyond. His thoughts drifted to the twins of Parros, Rinda and Remus, and he found himself hoping that the coming change would be for the better.

Shaking off his thoughtful lethargy, Guin strode forward again, ready to spring into battle should any danger come. But he remained preoccupied, pondering the future that lay before him.

The two tireless travelers made good time up the remainder of the slope, and soon they reached the pass where the two jutting ears pressed in from both sides. The tops of the ears were pointed so sharply that no man, wolf, or even mountain goat could have had a hope of scaling them. Yet though the ear-crags stuck out higher than where the wolf and the leopard-man now stood, it was apparent that for all means and purposes they had reached the summit of the Dog's Head.

The sun was nearing the zenith, casting its scalding rays down the path on the western slope along which they had climbed. Its burning glare was merciless upon their faces, and Guin and the Wolf King stopped to rest. Guin took the lizard skin that he had hung from his belt and chewed on it. It was as dry and tough as well-smoked jerky, but went well with the juice from the few cactus pods he had saved from his breakfast, which he now broke open between his teeth.

From the jagged peak they had a commanding view of their surroundings. It was not what most men would call a handsome vista; to search for scenery that met human standards of beauty would have been a bleak exercise in futility, for there was nothing to please the eye or lift the spirits in all the cruel miles they could see. It was a grim, inhuman sight that stretched out below them.

To the east, the ears of the Dog's Head blocked their view of the main ridgeline of the Kanan range. Gazing elsewhere they could see the winding path they had climbed and, below that and beyond on every side, an endless white sea of sand. Not a speck of green was visible, no patch of brush marred the even sands. The sky was free of clouds and vapors, and also of angel hair, for the wispy white ghost tendrils did not fall at this altitude.

It was a sight to which the Wolf King was long accustomed, and already it was becoming familiar to Guin as well. Nor did its sheer emptiness stir fear in the leopard-man's heart, for such emotions were useless to the wild denizens of the desert, and in the depths of his heart Guin was as wild as any other beast that roamed Nospherus. For a long moment wolf and warrior stood in the cool wind at the peak; then, rapidly, they began their descent.

Guin soon realized that the way down would be, if anything, more difficult than their climb up the mountain. The rock of the eastern slope was fine and loose, devoid of animal trails or other packed soil that could safely be relied upon. Evidently the wolves did not often venture to this side of the Dog's Head. As the two wound their way down between the rocks, Guin's feet slid in the scree, and his boots found sharp rocks hidden beneath the dust.

Several times the stone beneath Guin's feet crumbled away, and each time he slid several motad down the slope before regaining his footing. On other occasions he stepped on a rock that seemed stable, only to have the dirt supporting it give way, loosening a slide of boulders that rolled down the slope to the valley far below with a terrible crashing sound as he scrambled to arrest his own descent.

The wolf seemed to fare better than Guin on the loose gravel, but he too did not move as freely as he had on the way up.

Some of the scree was too unstable to support even him, balanced on four feet though he was, and the valley below echoed repeatedly with the cacophony of boulders, rocks, and sand knocked free by boots and paws.

Indeed the downward journey took much longer than had the ascent, and the two companions were forced to stop frequently to rest their aching muscles. The sun spilled its heat down relentlessly upon them. From the crags far away, they could hear the plaintive howling of wolves on the wind.

Go east, over the Dog's Head...

Had he not heard Rinda's voice so clearly as he left the oasis the morning before, the leopard-headed warrior knew, he would have been running blindly now, desperately trying to reach an unknown destination. Nor would he have met the Wolf King who now led him along the secret path they followed and stood by his side against the dangers of the mountain.

The sun was beginning to set on the wearying second day of Guin's journey. His time was half spent, and he had yet to see a sign of the Lagon for whom he sought. Yet his plight could have been far worse; for had he not met with the cyclone and then the Wolf King, he might now only be starting to climb the western slope of the Dog's Head, tired from an exhausting trek across the sand. Guin never once doubted that he was heading in the right direction, but navigating the Dog's Head without the Wolf

King's aid would have cost him dear time—time he would need to convince the Lagon to join him and the Sem in their struggle.

Nor could Guin have asked the Sem for more than four days in which to complete his mission. The wildlings were faced with a threat to their very existence, and he doubted that they could hold out even that long against an army of foes twice their number and twice their size as well. For all he knew, he might already be too late. The Mongauli force might have made its move that very morning. If they found the Sem and made a full-on assault... Then even if Guin did find the Lagon and convince them to come, all his effort would be wasted, too little, too late, a scant smattering of rain drops on the parched desert.

Two more days...

Guin did his best not to let his worry dangerously hasten his careful pace, but his fists clenched with suppressed tension as he thought of the impossibility of his task. The Wolf King looked up inquisitively. The sun was setting.

Carefully now the warrior and the wolf hurried onward. Darkness began to fall, long shadows stretching and joining around them; yet, by the time true night had arrived the two travelers had passed the dangerously steep crags and were walking along a gently sloping path that ran along the top of a cliff on the skirt of the mountain.

The wolf stopped, as if to suggest that they rest for the night where they were, but Guin was unwilling to pause now that he was over the obstacle of the mountain. At the same time, though the grade was gentler here, the ground was still loose and crumbling, and the cliff on their right hand dropped into a deep ravine. Where the path narrowed, a misstep on the shoulder would send rocks tumbling down into the dark abyss. The darker the path got, the more dangerous it would become.

The Wolf King, choosing his footing with utmost care, looked back at Guin, wordlessly requesting him to stop. Guin, however, was engrossed in his own progress, stabilizing himself with a firm grip on the boulders they passed, keeping a sharp eye out for stone-mimics and vampire moss as he made his way along the sloping cliff-edge. Seeing his companion's determination, the Wolf King faced forward again and continued down, his pace quickening.

Both Guin and the wolf had an advantage over the common traveler in that their eyes could see fairly well in the darkness. But then, they were walking on paths where no common traveler would ever think of venturing. *I would like to see Rinda and Remus brave this trail,* Guin thought, amusement flashing briefly through his mind. *Or even the intrepid Istavan—*

Abruptly he stopped, the hair on the back of his neck rising.

"What's that?" he barked.

The Wolf King did not slow his pace.

There was something ahead of them, something pure white, glimmering in the darkness.

Snow?

Guin squinted to see through the gloom.

Yidoh? Or something worse?

A short distance further on, the path dropped sharply. Beyond the drop he could dimly see faint white shapes that seemed to float in the void. His eyes could detect no movement, but he suspected that something lay ahead which he had not encountered before, so different was this pale gleaming from the monotonous gray of the mountainside that had filled his eyes for the past day and night.

Guin hesitated, his pace faltering. Then he shouted with alarm as the Wolf King sped up and launched himself through the air towards the strange cluster of white objects.

"Wait!"

The leopard warrior knew all too well that there were creatures in Nospherus that were neither plant, nor animal, nor mineral, unnatural entities that used nefarious means to lure in their prey, employing attractive scents or even psychic temptation. It was unwise to leap into the unknown no matter how safe it might look.

But the Wolf King moved like lightning, hopping down over the rocks; in an instant he was among the shapeless white *things*, stopping right on top of the closest one. To Guin's amazement, he crouched and began to lick his peculiar perch.

Guin's eyes flashed. Cautiously, but as quickly as he could manage, he moved down the last stretch of path along the cliff until he, too, was surrounded by the white lumps. He could now see that they were rocks of some sort, ranging from quite small to boulder-sized, lying scattered among the darker stones below the cliff. The area was covered with white dust that appeared to have fallen off the white rocks, making the ground look like a late autumn field after a snow flurry.

Guin stopped, watching the Wolf King in astonishment. The wise elder of Dog's Head Mountain had gone mad. Like a cat bewitched by catnip, he twisted his face in ecstasy as he rubbed against the pale rocks, and rolled on the ground, stopping from time to time to lick their surfaces again. The rocks were as white as the wolf's own fur, and they seemed fragile enough for his teeth to leave marks in them, dusting the ground with more pallid powder.

Guin gritted his teeth in dubious anticipation and reached out to touch one of the rocks. Nothing happened. He broke off a chunk and it crumbled easily in his hand; soon his palm was covered with the stuff. He glanced at the Wolf King. On closer inspection, the wolf appeared less crazed than he had seemed before. Rather, he was apparently merely enjoying himself tremendously. After a moment's hesitation, Guin brought his palm closer to his face, and sticking out his tongue, he lightly licked the powder.

"Ah ha!"

It was tangy, or rather salty—pleasantly so—a welcome treat for the mouth after a long day spent sweating under the dry desert sun.

"Rock salt," Guin muttered, astounded. He quickly moved to one of the largest rocks and broke off a chunk, testing it. It was as salty as the first. He looked around. As far as he could tell in the dark, the small valley they had entered was filled with white lumps of salt—more than he had ever seen in his life.

—— 4 ——

A low growl spilled from Guin's mouth. "White rocks…"

"Where the white stones dance upon the black mountain…"
In a flash, the words of Rinda's prediction filled his mind.
"The white rocks, the black mountain. She spoke of this place!"

Here beneath the towering night-shadow of the Dog's Head,
the fall of salty boulders was spread along the narrow valley, each
white mass gleaming in stark contrast with the ash-dark ground
on which it rested.

The Wolf King seemed to have completely forgotten about
his leopard-headed companion. He darted around, snorting
like an excited wolf cub, licking eagerly at the rocks. With his
white fur he looked like a large slab of rock salt himself, come to
life in the shape of a wolf.

Guin took a chunk of the white rock in his hand and thrust
it into his pocket. Then he picked up another, slightly smaller
piece and allowed himself to indulge in the salt. Rock salt was a

rare prize in the Nospherus desert. The Sem went to great lengths to obtain the large quantities of salt that they needed to survive in the exhausting climate, getting what they could from what meat they could find and culling the rest from their own fur when their sweat evaporated. He imagined how they would rejoice if they could see the natural wealth that now lay before him, but the thought distracted him for no more than an instant. He was not here to find salt; he was here for the Lagon.

"There you will find the soul of the Lagon," she said. Where are they?

Guin looked around. The night was already deep, and Aeris cast her pale light down from the star-spattered vault of the sky. The valley of rock salt glowed softly in the moonlight, like a northern vale dusted with a layer of fine snow.

With this amount of salt on the ground, and so little rain, this valley must be particularly unsuited for vegetation, Guin thought. His eyes searched for and did not find a single blade of grass or patch of moss. Nor could the leopard-man see any desert lizards flitting fleetly from rock to rock, nor any stone-mimics on their rocky perches. It seemed that no life of any kind inhabited the valley—certainly not the legendary giants whom he sought.

Yet Rinda prophesied that I would find the Lagon "over the Dog's Head, where the white stones dance upon the black mountain." This must be the place! But what did she mean by "soul of the Lagon"? And the death-wind?

Guin believed the truth of Rinda Farseer's prediction. Here were the white stones over the Dog's Head to prove it. Yet, even the best visions had a way of misleading even the best seers.

Wait. She said, "Beyond the white rock." I must have to pass through this valley first to find this Lagon-soul.

His path was clear, then. He must walk straight through the rock salt valley. Thankfully, it did not seem to go on for too great a distance.

Guin bit once more at the chunk of salt in his hand, but restrained himself from eating all of it. If he gave in to his desire for salt now, he would earn himself painful thirst later. He threw the chunk down upon the ground. It struck another of the salt rock boulders and split in two with a crack.

Hmm? Guin's sharp eyes fell upon something shiny. The chunk he threw had knocked a corner off one of the bigger rocks, and where it was broken he could see something buried in the stone. It glinted in the moonlight more brightly than the salt.

Swiftly he crouched and rubbed at the crumbling boulder until more of the surface fell away beneath his hand. His fingers found something hard there, something cold and metallic to the touch. It was buried deeper than he had thought, and no matter how hard he tugged at it he couldn't get it to budge.

Driven by an impulse he did not fully understand, Guin began scraping furiously at the boulder that held the object.

Whatever he had found, it was certainly peculiar. The portion protruding from the rock was silver-colored and smooth, with an unfamiliar shape. Again he tugged at it firmly but it still held fast. Scrabbling furiously at the boulder, he dug away enough of the salt until he could grab onto the object with both hands; then he pulled with all his strength, and finally it lifted out of the white rock and into his hand.

The thing was much smaller than he had imagined. He brushed the dust from it, and tilted his head as he held it up to the moonlight. He had seen nothing like it, and had no idea what it might be used for. He could tell, however, that it was some sort of tool, an object made for some purpose. It looked like a long silver whistle, or a prayer stick; perhaps it was a collapsible cane. Strange small nodules like the bumps on the back of a desert lizard ran along one side of it, glinting faintly.

Guin examined the object for a while longer, but further study revealed nothing more about it than he had initially observed. The lurking knowledge that hid in his wayward memory, which so often seemed to help him out of fixes and answer obscure questions did not aid him now. Yet the impulse that had told him to dig the object from the boulder now led him to thrust it into his belt.

I'll figure out later what this is for.

He looked around. "In any case," he muttered, "I need to cross this valley while Aeris still shines. If I intend to make my appointment with the Sem, I need to be heading back over the Dog's Head by noon tomorrow."

He looked over at the Wolf King, but the great beast remained utterly unconcerned with Guin. He had finished his wild frolicking in the salt, and now sat between two of the larger white stones, his tongue lolling out and a dazed look on his face, like that of a man who had been too long in his cups. His sharp eyes were half-closed, and his mouth was twisted into a grimace that, were he human, would have made him look much like a grinning fool. Despite the impatience he had shown as he led Guin over the mountain, following some unspoken schedule that needed to be kept, he now seemed to have completely lost interest in their journey.

Or perhaps Guin had been wrong to hope that the wolf, as clever as he might be, had been sent on a mission, divinely inspired or otherwise, to lead him. It was possible that the Wolf King had just wanted to come to this rock salt valley, which to him held the same magic as catnip holds for a cat or wine for a thirsty man, and had only stayed with Guin until they reached it.

Still, the leopard-man felt that it was too early for them to part ways just yet. He felt a spiritual link with this wolf, his stalwart companion for a day and a night. Yet when he called out, the Wolf King only turned his lazy eyes toward him, shooting him an annoyed look. He clearly had no intention of going any further.

"I see," sighed Guin after trying a few more times to rouse the wolf's attention. "It is here that we part, then. I won't forget your help. If I do bring back the Lagon, I will be crossing back over this mountain, and passing through your kingdom again. But I do not think we will meet if I come leading an army of giants, will we?"

He spoke as though the wolf could understand him. There was indeed a deep connection between the giant white wolf-lord of Dog's Head Mountain and the leopard-headed warrior who bore a great burden of destiny. It was a deeper tie than that of friendship or even kinship. Guin was reluctant to leave his savior behind.

Shooting a last farewell glance at the lupine king who sat complacently on his throne of salt, the leopard-man strode out into the middle of the valley. The moonlight made the rock salt stones appear to float above the valley floor, and the reflected light from the salt crystals lit his path as though it were day.

Guin moved with long sure strides. He turned around only once to look back toward his companion, but the Wolf King, having had his fill of salt, had apparently slipped away to find some water to drink—or perhaps his ancient fur, pale as the high Ashgarn glaciers, hid him among the white of the rock salt boulders. In any case he was nowhere to be seen.

Guin was alone once more.

Even though the great wolf was far from human and had been unable to share words with the leopard-warrior, a companion was a companion, and now Guin felt his absence. Without the great wolf by his side, the road seemed mirthless to him, and longer than it really was. For a while he feared that the trek through the valley of rock salt would never end. Yet soon that thought, too, was gone.

Guin quickened his pace and marched on. The scenery around him grew increasingly bizarre. Where he first entered the valley, the black soil of the ground beneath the salt had been revealed in many places, like a dark sea between the floating white bergs of salt. Now it was concealed entirely, lost under a solid sheet of white. Here and there, the salt had crystallized into beautiful, strangely shaped spires and mounds. Guin passed through a salt formation that appeared to be formed over and around the bones of some huge animal, thrusting up from the ground into the sky. Then, he strode between strange glowing trees of salt. He did not think the salt capable of killing outright, so he surmised that whatever had owned the bones had first died, then

been covered with salt crystals. The resulting sculpture was as chilling as it was beautiful. The trees were equally arresting. There was no less than a small copse of dead trees, all completely over-grown and consumed by the salt. It was a phantasmagorical sight, and unsettling when he thought on it too long.

The ground crunched softly underneath Guin's feet. The layer of salt was growing deeper as he neared the middle of the valley. Then his boot came down upon a perfectly formed sphere; it crushed beneath his weight and he saw something shine like a ruby from the shards. For a moment, he thought the salt ball was bleeding. Curiously he picked up the bright shape that his footfall had revealed.

Guin gasped. It was the pure red fruit of some plant. It had probably fallen from one of the salt-imprisoned trees and had become perfectly preserved. It was shiny like a gemstone. Given the encrustation on the trees he thought that it must be quite old, but encased as it was he doubted that it could have rotted. He took a tentative bite, but quickly spit it out. It tasted like pure salt; no trace of the fruit's flavor remained.

Suddenly this landscape, which had at first appeared beau-tiful and exotic to the leopard-man, began to seem threaten-ing, and a subtle fear crept into his heart. It was as if he had wandered into a painting of some faraway, unseen world, pleas-ing to the eye but hostile to life. There were no springs or rivers here, nor would any water here ever be drinkable. No fish or bigmouth from the Kes could ever come to these dry gullies; no moss would ever grow from these barren stones.

The salt sucked all the moisture out of the air. For a moment the delusion gripped Guin that if he were to misstep, twist his foot, and fall, the salt would flow into his mouth and rob the water from his body, transforming him in moments into a desiccated mummy. Then he would lie forever preserved in this snowfield of salt, a statue to be covered in time with beautiful white powder. This was a valley of death.

This, too, is Nospherus, a cursed land.

Guin growled. His throat was dry, perhaps because of the salt he had licked, perhaps because the insidious valley had steadily sucked the water from his body even as he walked across it.

I think I actually prefer the harsh sands of the open desert to this dead place.

After a time Guin noticed the air around him getting lighter, and he lifted his head and surveyed his surroundings. He realized with surprise that he had walked through the night in the strange white valley. At some point the dim light of Aeris had given way to the first ruddy light foretelling the arrival of Ruah's fiery chariot.

The third morning had dawned.

Two days left—and those two days begin now. I wonder if Is-

*tavan is carrying out his part of the plan. I hope the Sem haven't
split up and fallen to fighting amongst themselves. Are the twins
waiting as I told them to? How far have the Mongauli advanced?*

All these things he could not know. Guin looked up to the
sky for answers as the first rays of Ruah's burning orb reached the
dead valley. He jerked back as though he had been stricken. Hurriedly, he lifted a hand to ward off the furiously bright, pris-
matic light that assailed him from every direction.

The sun hit the salt and shone brighter than the brightest
snow. The salt trees and rocks, the jagged bones and even the
footprints that Guin had left behind caught the sun's light in
untold thousands of tiny crystals, and like a morning ceremony
at the Crystal Palace echoing with holy dirges, they blazed in a
symphony of rainbow light. Only, unlike the ceremonies of Parros, this display blazed so intensely that it seared.

It was excruciatingly beautiful, this dance of fearful bright-
ness, but its beauty gave the leopard-man no joy, for had he
gazed upon it for more than an instant, it might have scorched
the very eyes from his head. He found that he was unable to pro-
ceed even with his eyes tightly shut, feeling his way with outstretched hands; for even when his eyes were closed the terrible
light beat against his lids and slowly burned into his brain. Guin
stopped, uncertain of what to do. If the fierce blaze blinded
him, he would be stranded. Finally he covered both eyes with

his hands and pressed onward, feeling his way with his booted feet. He knew that if he just kept going straight he would soon be out of the salt-encrusted valley.

His pace acquired a new urgency now. He had to escape the unexpected menace of the burning light. Repeatedly he tripped over rocks that lay in his path and felt the salt sting in cuts on his knees and elbows, but each time he simply clambered to his feet again and kept on walking, heedless of the pain. He walked faster and faster, until he was almost running. Even with his eyes shut tightly there was one thing he could sense around him; it was a disembodied hatred, as palpable as the sun's light was blinding.

He ran.

He would have run right past the valley patrol, had a thick voice not sounded right in front of him.

"Stop!"

The voice sounded both alarmed and threatening. It was joined by other voices coming out of the white blindness.

"Stop. What are you doing?"

"Where are you going?"

"Who are you?"

Guin opened his eyes, braving the burning light. As soon as he lowered his hands he noticed that the reflected rays were much dimmer here; he was nearing the edge of the valley. Blinking and squinting, he peered ahead, and he saw them: four hulking shapes, towering in his path. He had found the Lagon at last.

The creatures had to be Lagon. What else could they be, but the giants of Nospherus? They stood blocking Guin's path, pointing great spears at him, the broad stone spearheads aimed straight at his chest. Though Guin himself was a good six taar high, the shortest of them was at least a finger taller, and the tallest stood a head above Guin.

The giants were proportionally broad, though they carried themselves with an ease that made them seem relatively light for their huge frames, and therefore swift and agile. They were all muscle and bone, lacking any excess weight. Judging from the quickness with which they handled their giant stone-tipped spears, they had considerable strength.

Those spears all remained pointed at Guin. Not one of the Lagon risked glancing away. Their wary eyes were filled with mistrust and bewilderment.

At first he thought they were all male, but then he noticed that the shortest of them was slightly different. She had to be a female. She was more lightly built, and had long hair that flowed down over her shoulders and across her chest. While the other three wore only leather loincloths, she wore a skin tunic that was tied at one shoulder and covered her torso and her legs down to the knee.

Aside from these details, however, she seemed little different from the others. All wore the same leather sandals, and all were hairy, though not so hairy as the Sem, at least on the front of their bodies. They seemed to have spread some sort of animal grease upon themselves, and their exposed skin was largely covered with gleaming smears of the stuff. Where their natural skin did show it was a deep coppery color. Their faces were entirely unlike those of the smaller residents of Nospherus; their foreheads were rather wide, and their jaws jutted out slightly, giving their heads an unbalanced look like wine jugs turned upside down. But their eyes were unmistakably intelligent, and they shone with violence. At their waists hung stone short swords, and they each seemed to carry a set of strange implements: a small bowl that looked like a rock with a hollow carved out of it, and a long-handled spoon.

"Who are you?" the tallest of the Lagon spoke again. "You have the head of a beast, but the body of a Lagon. I have not seen your kind. Who are you?"

Guin wondered how he should answer. Then amazement flashed through him as he realized that the miracles had not ceased, for he could understand the language of the Lagon. Its thick and deep tones were markedly different from the high-pitched squeaking of the Sem tongue, but the words were quite similar. Perhaps there was something to the legend that the Sem and the Lagon were both descendants of the people of Kanan and shared the same ancestral language and customs.

"I..." Guin coughed, still unsure of how he should introduce himself. He liked the way the language felt, though. His throat and chest were much better suited to its low tones.

"It speaks!" said one of the Lagon, spear still raised. "Is it Lagon?"

"No," said another, "no Lagon has the head of a beast!"

"But beasts do not talk," the first rejoined.

"And what manner of beast is it?" mused the third Lagon male. "It is not a wolf, or a lizard."

"If he can speak, he must be Lagon," said the first with finality. Having come to an agreement about the nature of the strange warrior, they thrust out their spears.

The one that had spoken first challenged Guin now, his voice threatening. "Lagon with the head of a beast, where did you come from?"

"My name is Guin," the leopard-man replied slowly. "I came through the valley of salt, from across the Dog's Head."

"Across the Dog's Head is the land of the dead," the Lagon answered. He seemed to be the leader of this party.

"But I am alive," said Guin. "Beyond the Dog's Head is not the land of the dead. I came here from over the mountain."

"Over the mountain is death!" the leader repeated obstinately. "That is why you have the head of a beast. You are an evil spirit, and you stole that head to walk among the living."

"No, it is my own head, and I am no spirit," the leopard-man insisted, exasperated at his inability to explain something that he did not understand himself. He changed his tack. "I have a request. I must meet your king."

His words seemed to have an odd effect on the Lagon. They looked at one another, and for a moment he thought they might not have understood him.

"Or do the Lagon have no king?" Guin asked.

"We have no king," replied the leader. "The sage Kah and the warrior Dodok decide all things for the Lagon."

"Then let me meet this sage Kah and this warrior Dodok."

"We will bring you before them," said the leader curtly, "as our prisoner. They will judge your punishment. You are a fiend from the land of the dead, and you have tread upon the sacred white sand."

Then he started, noticing the lump of salt in Guin's pocket. "What is this?" he demanded loudly, fishing the salt out with a swift hand. The white crystals crumbled onto the ground. "The white sand belongs to Lagon only. It is sacred to Lagon. Thieves must be punished. Come." He emphasized his words by stepping back and prodding Guin's chest with the tip of his spear.

Guin had no intention of quarreling. He was here to meet

the leaders of the Lagon, even if that meeting had to happen on such unfavorable terms. The four Lagon formed a watchful circle around him and urged him back the way that they had come, along the black earth of a gentle slope that led down and away from the rock salt valley. Silently the leopard-man followed their lead.

Guin was a prisoner of the Lagon.

Chapter Four

FIRE AND STONE

—— I ——

While the bizarre sandstorm that carried Guin to the Dog's Head two days before had hit the leopard-man straight on, only its whirling fringes had reached the Mongauli. Far to the south of the maelstrom's center, the invaders were never in great danger. The weather they faced was a mere pond-ripple compared to the tidal wave of sand that Guin had endured.

Still, even the storm's edge was enough to arrest the progress of the expeditionary army. The Mongauli hastily picked a location suitable for a temporary encampment, and moments later they had erected the lady general's tent and begun preparing for a long wait. The soldiers brought out the horse blankets they used as bedding and stretched the coarse fabric over makeshift frames, and under these barely adequate shelters they weathered the howling winds and the hail of dirt and stones.

The men huddled together, cursing their misfortune in hushed tones so that the officers would not hear them.

"What a place this is!" a young knight of Mongaul muttered, shaking his head. "What could this accursed domain of fiends possibly hold that's worth all this suffering?"

"Quiet, now. Are ye suggesting we rebel against our captain?" said another who knelt nearby under the dubious shelter of the tarp they shared.

"No, no, I'm not rebelling. I'm just thinking. Listen to that wind howling like a demon! Listen to the sand and stones raining on that blanket! This is no place for men to live. I've just about had it."

"And ye think I like it? We're soldiers of Mongaul. We're to give our *lives* to Mongaul!"

"I'm ready to fight and die for Mongaul, sure. There's not one could call me a coward—and you know it. But I can think of plenty of better ways to die than being buried in a sandstorm, or getting sucked dry by one of them blood-sucking monsters out there. That's a dog's death, that is. No way for any warrior to go, let alone a proud soldier of Mongaul."

"Ye're right, there. Pity poor Captain Leegan, so young, so brave. To get yer very life drawn out of ye through yer skin by those nasty yidoh!"

"Is that what we're going to tell Count Ricard when we get back, I wonder? That Viscount Leegan was swallowed by a creeping porridge?"

"All I know is I don't want to be the one to tell him. Aye, this is a right horrible place. This whole cursed land should be burned in Doalfire and go back to the charred hell it came from. And those Sem and that leopard-headed freak along with it."

"See, you feel the same way about this place as I do." The younger knight seemed almost pleased he had company in his misery. "Listen to that horrid sound, it's riding on the wind. What is that?"

"Desert wolves howling!" spat another knight behind him.

"I tell you I hate this place, I hate it."

The storm raged for three *twists* of the sand clock. When it had blown by at last, night was falling. The Mongauli crept from their shelters to review the damage.

Several soldiers and their horses had been dragged down into sandy graves by the bigmouths, sand leeches, and mouths-of-the-desert that had emerged suddenly from the dunes while the winds were raging. The men who were nearest the victims had tried to save their comrades, reaching out desperate hands, tossing ropes and throwing spears, but they had been well nigh helpless in the ferocity of the storm. Just looking into the gale had been enough to blind a man with driving sand. Yet even during the brief lulls in the wind they were not safe; during one moment of quiet, a section of ground towards the middle of the makeshift camp had suddenly split open, and from the chasm the sickening pale white tentacles of a mouth-of-the-desert had come snaking, hunting for food. The sand around the mouth had then become a funnel, sucking in four or five soldiers in the blink of an eye. Crazed, the lost soldiers' companions had slashed at the swirling tentacles, trying desperately to avoid the downward rush of sand. Then, although it was midday, the skies had darkened again, and in the howling darkness the desert was once again revealed to be a hellish realm of monsters ravaging unchecked.

The losses during the storm were more demoralizing than any of the Sem raids had been. There was even less that the Mongauli could do about them. Thankfully, however, the harsh weather had also kept the Sem from moving, and so the rest of the day passed without a single sign of the enemy.

Now, as the Mongauli officers continued to survey the damage that the storm had done, night came down around them. At every other night camp, they had directed the soldiers to pound down the sandy soil in a wide circumference around their bivouac, making sure there were no nests of harmful animals or plants concealed nearby, but tonight they had not had the luxury of a choice of camping grounds. All the men knew this, and realized that even though the storm was gone they could not be certain of the safety of their surroundings. Still, the departure of the howling wind from their ears and the dancing sand from their eyes improved their mood considerably. When the cold, star-studded sky finally showed itself above them, the men relaxed, too tired even to worry about the wildlings. Rations were distributed, and the scouts went out on their rounds.

Throughout the sandstorm, the captains had been engaged in a council of war in the general's pavilion. At last, well after the sands had settled, a servant's hand drew back the tent flap, and the captains shuffled out and returned to their men.

No sooner had Count Marus, with his lieutenant Garanth in tow, arrived at the campsite of the blue knights from Tauride than his personal guard and staff hurried up, Eru of Argon among them.

"What news from the war council, Lord Captain?" Eru asked before any of the others could speak.

Count Marus nodded to the young knight without replying and looked his officers over. "Give your men double rations, then have them sleep in two alternating watches, with their weapons at the ready. Tomorrow morning we make our move at last."

"Our move, Captain?"

"We are through letting the Sem dictate the terms of this engagement. For the past few days we have fought this battle warily, not wanting to make the mistake that Leegan Corps made of following the wildlings too closely, lest we fall into another of their traps. And so we bore their raids without striking back. However, I have convinced our Lady that there is nothing for us to gain through this over-cautious strategy. In the morning, we are to take action."

Garanth continued for his lord. "Tomorrow, when the sun rises, we will bring an end to this conflict. Should the Sem come on another raid, we will meet them head-on, and pursue them relentlessly when they retreat. Then we will search out their nest and exterminate the foul monkeys. Have heart, men! Tomorrow, we go hunting!"

The troop leaders cheered. Without waiting for orders, they ran off to deliver the news to their respective commands. In a short while, cheers rose from groups of men throughout the camp.

To a man, the Mongauli had grown weary of their constant defense against the Sem. Now, the entire expeditionary force was on its feet, ready to move, like a lion that had wakened after a long sleep and was now stretching its muscles to ready for a hunt. The soldiers had barely set camp and already they seemed impatient for the night to finish. From here and there rose the sound of horses whinnying and men talking and laughing and the clang of sword upon sword as the most avid officers staged impromptu practice drills. Liveliness filled the Mongauli camp.

Eru of Argon lingered near Count Marus, seemingly unwilling to leave. He caught the count's eye and sauntered over, speaking in his characteristic familiar tone.

"Lord Captain. Congratulations."

Oddly enough, even though his suggestion to attack the Sem had been adopted by the war council, Count Marus did not seem as pleased as he might be. But when he saw Eru's friendly black eyes sparkling, he smiled. "Eru, you jest. What is there to congratulate when we have yet to join battle?"

"Oh? Was this general attack not m'lord captain's suggestion? Since everyone agreed with you, and the general favored you with the lead position tomorrow, I would think that's more than reason enough for congratulations."

"Well, yes, perhaps. I suppose I should stop worrying."

The youthful Eru's words had a way of warming up the count's cold heart. If he had been a younger captain, he might have thought Eru presumptuous, but for Count Marus, the knight's attitude and brazen style of speech reminded him of his eldest son, whom he had not seen in many years—the Viscount Maltius, far away in the city of Torus. Count Marus scanned the camp around them, looking for Garanth, but his faithful lieutenant had gone off to see that the men were prepared for the march in the morning.

"Worrying, m'lord? What troubles you?"

"That sandstorm, Eru. When the council began, I suggested that we move on the Sem right now, this very moment. Now that the storm has lasted into nightfall, we are forced to sit here on our haunches waiting for them to come to us. That will have a negative impact on our morale. It would be far better to strike out at the Sem first, and force the battle at our pace, not theirs. But night is here, and like it or not we must camp again. Our attack must wait until the next morning, and more time passes."

"I'm sure that, in the morning, the Sem will still be out there. We can launch our attack then. And there can't be more than five or six *twists* left till full light comes again."

"No, the Sem will not disappear. But if I were a Sem, and I knew well the tides of battle, I would not attack at all tomorrow. I would not even let the enemy catch a glimpse of me for a full day at least. No, I would give the Mongauli host the cold shoulder. Let them simmer, that is what I'd do. Sometimes the hardest thing to endure in war is to have one's spirit soar and then have to wait, unable to launch an attack when morale is at its highest. But that's just speculation, and we'll find a way to harness the energy of our men. When morning comes, scouts will go in all directions to look for the main Sem force, and I'm sure they will find them, and all will be well."

Marus sighed and looked out into the night sky, as though

he could will Ruah's chariot to race faster and bring the morning now. "You know, Eru, it may sound foolish, but what really troubles me is the poor timing of the storm. It is almost as though it knew we were ready to move and it came to stop us."

"Well, the timing was ill, I agree, but I'm afraid it's just coincidence, m'lord captain," said Eru, smiling easily. "You don't think the Sem had anything to do with the storm, do you, m'lord? I know the monkeys are crafty, but they're no wind-mages!"

Marus smiled at the jest, but then a serious look drifted over his face. He put his arm on Eru's shoulder, the teacher speaking to his trusted pupil. "In battle, it is of utmost importance that a commander be alert and watchful, able to read the tides of the conflict. But even more importantly, Eru, he must be able to *sense* the shifting of the engagement. A battle is a living thing, a capricious, feral animal. You never know which of a thousand factors might change its snarling face. Any little thing could. Weather, coincidence, these things might have a greater pull on the outcome of combat than any choice made by a commander. The battle lives and breathes; you can *feel* it on your skin. Generals that do not know this, Eru..." Marus shook his head. "You can read all the books of Alzandross and still only be 'well educated.' Education does not make you a general, or a leader of men."

"I will remember what you have said," Eru assured him, his tone thoughtful. "But, I fear you worry too much, Lord Captain. If the weather was truly on the side of the Sem, they surely would have come at us under cover of the storm, and in the absence of any such attack, our morale has soared to its highest yet. By sundown tomorrow, all dues will be paid, and the leaders of our army will be the undisputed lords of Nospherus."

"I hope you are right," said Marus, clapping a hand on Eru's shoulder. He seemed to have completely forgotten that the man next to him was Eru of Argon, and not his son, the viscount. "Ah, I am getting old—so easily worried."

The count sighed. The darkened dunes glittered in the light of the Mongauli watchfires, their white sands unmarred by any shadow of approaching Sem raiders. "I wonder," he said wistfully, "if I'll ever see the watchtower of Tauride Castle reflected white in the blue water again. I've never had such a thought before this campaign, not in the hardest of battles. But since heading out on our Nospherus expedition, this feeling of impending doom has come to me a hundred times. I wonder if I'll ever see again the Golden Scorpion Palace shining in splendor above the streets of Torus, or the black lion of Gohra and the golden scorpion of Mongaul flying proudly from the Tower of the Five Kings. Will I ever again see my son, sent to serve in the army in Torus, at the age of sixteen? He will be twenty this year, finished with his obligation to the Palace Guard, and given a captain's flag like Astrias or young Leegan..."

The count's voice faded. Eru stood quietly looking up at his weathered face. The knight's black eyes shone with a mysterious light.

Marus emerged from his reverie and smiled at Eru. "You should go," he said, raising his hand. "Go and prepare for the coming march. Do not worry. Mongaul will not lose this battle. Even should this old man not see Tauride or Torus again, you hardy youths will return to the homeland as heroes."

Eru looked again at Marus with that same inexplicable expression on his face, then turned and quietly walked back to his horse. He seemed to have no trouble putting his captain's worries out of his mind as he hunched down beside his steed, slid into his bedroll and fell deeply asleep. If the general attack was going to begin in the morning, he needed to get some rest, even if only a little. The other men seemed to have gradually come to the same conclusion, and save for occasional stirring, the entire Mongauli army was now quiet, bedded down for the night.

Before the first light of dawn began to paint the sky red, the soldiers were up and active, eating their morning's rations. The weariness of the long march was fading from their dust-covered faces, wiped away by the knowledge that soon all their efforts would be rewarded. Foremost in their thoughts was the implacable Guin. At that very moment the leopard-man was facing the long ascent of the Dog's Head with the ancient Wolf King; but the Mongauli army had no way of knowing this. The invaders thought that Guin was still with the Sem, planning fiendish strategies, and it fueled their hatred of him all the more. They quietly dreamed that today would be the day they hung his head on a spear before their camp and toasted his death around the campfire.

By the time the first rays of sunlight flooded the desert from the eastern sky, all of the five thousand knights and five thousand footsoldiers and crossbowmen who remained to the Mongauli army were prepared for battle, lined up by their squads. The squads, in turn, now moved their ranks to stand behind their leaders, who brought each group of knights in massive formation behind the captains of the red, blue, black, and white knights. The four hues of armor reflected off the white sands of Nospherus in a dazzling array of color. They had forgotten that their number had been reduced by a third from what it had been when they crossed the banks of the Kes. Forgotten, too, were the injuries that plagued many of those who remained, the constant thirst that rattled in their throats, and the insufferable white grit that had found its way into their armor, their helmets, and their clothes, rendering every moment a discomfort. The

Gohran warriors were as exuberant as they had been on the first day of the expedition—full of life, and ready for battle.

"Quiet! Order in the ranks!" the captains' voices lifted up above the clattering of arms and armor. Gradually, even the whinnying of the horses was stilled, and silence pervaded the formation. Then a great cheer went up. Amnelis, Lady of Mongaul and commander of the expeditionary force, had appeared.

"Long live the Lady General!"

"Long live the General of the Right!"

A dais had been raised in front of the pavilion and atop it she stood, tall and majestic. From her vantage point she could see and be seen by the entire army. Her trusted aides Vlon and Lindrot stood guard to either side, almost lost in the glare of the morning light which blazed off Amnelis's pure white armor. Yet even more brilliant than her jewel-studded armor was the golden waterfall of hair that flowed from her helmless head down over her shoulders.

The assembled army fell silent. To the Mongauli soldiers, Amnelis was no less than a goddess of victory, come to life to walk among them, to lead them on to glory. A fair and noble beauty she was, and yet mighty as any battle-hardened knight, and she held them entranced. Every eye was focused on her.

"Brave warriors of Mongaul!"

Her voice was clear and sharp, seeming to soar over their

heads, reaching to the far corners of the desert.

"You have been most patient. And I believe you have grown tired of waiting for the Sem. The wait is over! Soldiers, take up your swords! We shall no longer fear this land of Nospherus. What can be more fitting for the brave corps of Mongaul than a glorious attack? We will strike at the Sem tribes, kill the wildlings, and raise the flag of the Golden Scorpion across this desert land!"

From ten thousand mouths the cheers roared out, shaking the dunes.

"Long live the Lady General!"

"Glory for Mongaul!"

Amnelis listened with an air of satisfaction. Then, with her long cloak sweeping behind her, she sprang lightly from her dais to the ground, ignoring the short steps her attendants had prepared for her. The white knight Feldrik approached.

"Feldrik!" she called to him.

"Yes, my lady!"

"Once preparations are complete, we will march at once. If we linger here too long and let the Sem attack us, the troops' spirits will ebb. Lead the army east according to plan, and when the Sem show themselves, hit them with all our power and destroy them. And do not forget to send out the scouts. We must find their villages."

"I understand and obey," Feldrik replied, saluting crisply.

"One more thing," Amnelis said. "Marus Corps will ride in the vanguard. Send orders to the count to move at once. And inform Astrias that he will have the rearguard."

"Very well, my lady."

Amnelis nodded. "I will go prepare now." The lady general strode away, her hair lifting and curling in the breeze as though it had a life of its own. It shone as it floated in the desert air behind her. Feldrik watched her go. She was truly beautiful.

Truly a sight for sore eyes. But this is a harsh expedition, with no time or room for comforts, and yet, one full squad of footsoldiers under the white knights' command is needlessly burdened with this princess's soft bed and sheets, her changes of clothes, and her food. And though we are in the middle of the desert her white gloves and boots do not have a speck of dust upon them. How many days' worth of drinking water does it take to wash that hair, I wonder?

Amnelis glanced back unexpectedly and Feldrik, flustered, whirled and hurried off to give his orders. She may have looked soft and feminine, but in all other ways she was as harsh and hard as the desert itself, and few knew this better than Feldrik.

As the rest of the army finished making its preparations, Marus Corps had slowly begun to move like a giant blue snake slithering across the sand. Here and there they passed traces of fires from the night camp, left among discarded trash and broken equipment that had been tossed aside. They were the pursuers now. There was no need to cover up signs of their passage.

Seeing the lead riders begin to move, Eru of Argon hurriedly mounted and moved into formation. He still held the remnants of his breakfast in his hand, a lump of dried vasya fruit at which he gazed with evident distaste. "This vasya's been cursed by Doal, no doubt," he grumbled, loud enough for the knights around him to hear. "It's terribly bitter, and it pricks the tongue. What are the rations officers thinking, handing out this stuff?"

"It's 'cause it's dried," observed an older knight who rode nearby, smirking. "We can't get fresh-picked vasya from Odain out here, you know."

"If it's that foul, throw it out," grunted another.

Eru grimaced, and continued to stare at the fruit disparagingly for a while, seemingly reluctant to cast away even an awful meal when so little food was available. When the lines around him began to move, he finally gave up on it and threw it at a campfire which was still smoldering near at hand.

The discarded fruit seemed to be very dry indeed. As soon as it hit the fire, it made a small popping noise and split open, sending up a line of smoke. The smoke became a beautiful orange snake, wending up into the blue sky.

"What's this?" Eru exclaimed with a shocked look. "That's

no vasya fruit. It's smokegrass root! I'd have died if I'd eaten that! Now I know the rations officers are in league with Doal!"

"Must have been one of the signal packets got mixed up with the supplies!" said his companions, guffawing and trying to calm down the indignant Eru. The smoke rose in great plumes from the fire.

"Hey, somebody better throw some water on it and put out that signal-smoke," Eru remarked grouchily. "The enemy'll see our position! Some water..."

Everyone hurriedly looked away. Nobody wanted to waste a precious drop of water out here. It was the only thing keeping them from death in this desert.

"Ah leave it," said one of the blue knights who had ridden up from the back of the column. "One of the footmen will kick some sand on it. And who cares if the Sem find us? By Doal's filthy beard, if they see that smoke and come running it will save us the trouble of going to find 'em!" The knight chuckled and waved Eru forward. They were already falling behind the others.

A troop commander saw the smoke and came over to ask what had happened, but when he heard, he laughed and let it be. The smokegrass had almost burned itself out by that time anyway.

The Mongauli army was in no mood to fret about a little accident with a campfire. From the officers down to the lowliest of footsoldiers, all were filled with eagerness and courage. There was a noticeable spring in each man's step, and even the horses seemed more spirited than usual. The only one without a smile on his face was Count Marus, and he hid his scowl behind his faceplate. Around him, the soldiers sang songs of Mongaul in loud voices as they marched.

Fearlessly the army advanced into the desert, leaving the orange smoke to rise behind them like a twisting Danayn water snake floating high into the empty heavens.

——— 2 ———

One *twist* later, the Sem tribes fell upon the eagerly advancing Mongauli army. This time, the Mongauli were ready. Their hands unbound, free to return the Sem attack and keep pushing, their spirits were high, and the thought of battle only increased their morale.

"The Sem come!"

A sentry posted on the ridge of a dune just ahead of the foremost riders saw a thin line of dust rising from the shadow on the dune's far side and quickly raised the alarm. The response from the men was immediate and enthusiastic.

"We've found them!"

"Finally!"

"Our friends have returned!"

"Tonight we feast, men!"

Shouts rose throughout the formation.

"Keep your voices down. The Sem might suspect something," one of the knights called out, warily thumbing the hilt of his sword.

"Nonsense," replied a companion riding nearby. "We'll cut those tiny heads off those furry necks before they know what's hit them!"

"That's right! For Captain Leegan!"

"Revenge! Revenge!"

Their hearts stirring with anticipation of the coming battle, the knights lowered their faceplates and rechecked the edges of their blades, while the crossbowmen spread out and made sure that their quivers were ready to hand. As they prepared, the cloud of dust rising from beyond the dune-ridge grew larger and began to spread, as if it would engulf the Mongauli host entirely.

"Well, it seems the Sem mean business this time. Looks like there's a lot of them," one of the blue knights remarked, watching the dust cloud that revealed their enemy's movements as it shifted in the morning wind.

"Nonsense!" replied another. "No matter how many of them come, they've certainly not got three times our number! And even if they did, that would just mean that once each of us wrings three monkey necks a piece we'll be out of enemies!" The knight laughed raucously at his own jest.

"Watch the poison arrows," his friend noted grimly, checking the fit of his neckpiece.

The Mongauli soldiers did not know that the combined forces of the Raku, Guro, Tubai, and Rasa added up to less than half the number of the invaders. Lacking the aid of the Karoi tribe, who were as big and as strong as the Raku and better warriors, the Sem army had suffered heavy losses over the course of its raids, and the wildling ranks were dwindling. The Sem had done what they could to keep this fact a secret from the Mongauli, sending out women and youths in each skirmish as decoys to raise dust clouds and conceal the warriors' true position and strength.

It made little difference to the Mongauli today, however. The men were flushed red with a fierce determination to meet the crafty monkeys in battle and kill every last one of them, be they one hundred or one hundred thousand.

The messengers ran down the lines, transmitting orders from Amnelis's central command. Once again, the host spread out like a flower blooming. Black, blue, and red petals extended from a white center. The crossbowmen moved to the outer ranks, with the footmen spreading out among them to defend them when the enemy closed in. The knights swiftly formed into several lines behind the front defenses and calmed their horses with soft voices and gestures, waiting their turn.

"Aii, aii, aiiie!"

The wildling war cry seemed to erupt from the sand all

around the Mongauli. It was soon followed by the Sem tribes themselves, appearing at the top of the gently sloping dunes in a half-circle formation that threatened the center and both flanks of the invaders' army.

"And so the monkeys have come."

Count Marus glared at the Sem horde above them. He still had his faceplate raised, to get a better view of the dunes, and the ragged white hair and beard that protruded from beneath his blue helm shone brilliantly in the sun and wind.

"Lord Captain, Lord Captain! Please, lower your visor!" Garanth exclaimed, fearing that his lord would make a perfect target for the Sem poison arrows. Marus quickly lowered his faceplate, but before the blue-painted iron mask covered his captain's eyes, Garanth noticed the worry reflected within them as they stared at the tiny wildlings atop the dunes.

"We need but a *twist* to rout them," the lieutenant said soothingly.

"Garanth," said the count, turning toward him.

"Yes, Lord Captain?"

"Do not die today." Perhaps the count meant to add: *Not here in this sandy hell.*

Garanth laughed. He was about to respond when the Sem began to charge down the dune like an avalanche, without order or formation, raising a wild cry as they hurtled toward the Mongauli lines. The battle was joined.

The sun blazed hot and white in the sky, searing the tops of the dunes, baking the men and wildings below. The method of battle was a familiar one for both armies. Though the Gohran army's spirits were higher than ever before, this was, after all, another clash of a kind that had grown grimly monotonous over the past few days, and they had no new position or strategy to make this one any different from all the rest.

The Mongauli crossbowmen in the front ranks loosed flights of shot that sent up puffs of white dust where they hit the sand and knocked over the Sem they struck. Then, as soon as the enemy drew near, the crossbowmen retreated behind the lines of the foot-soldiers and took cover. The infantry layered their shields and crouched down low, slowly advancing while protecting themselves from the poison arrows of the wildlings.

The Sem charged down the dunes, giving a tremendous war cry as they came. They were a mob, with no discernable order or strategy; their faces were painted with evil colors in garish patterns, the traditional marks of the wildling warriors, and their eyes blazed with crazed ferocity. They held blowpipes in their hands which they put to their mouths as they ran, interrupting their yells just long enough to fire volleys of tiny black arrows. Not pausing to aim, they could only hope that a few of the missiles would strike chinks in the Mongauli's armor so that the poison could do its deadly work.

When they had drawn so near to their foes that they no longer had time to reload their weapons as they ran, they slung the tubes into the netting that they wore on their backs and drew out stone axes for the melee. Then like a storm the Sem crashed into the ranks of the human footmen, the nimble wildings running up the overlapping shields of the infantry as if they were climbing ladders, vaulting high and then descending among the ranks of men to strike at them with their axes.

Some of the footmen, who had learned to anticipate this tactic by now, were able to use their shields to knock the vaulting Sem back. Others thrust out spears between the shields, skewering wildling warriors in mid-flight. But where their first assault was stymied, the Sem quickly joined hands to form living springboards and sent their companions flying over the front row of soldiers, until everywhere inside the lines was a frenzy of deadly hand-to-hand combat.

The footsoldiers dropped their shields and whirled around, drawing their swords to meet the first wave of Sem even as more of the wildlings came down the dunes in an avalanche of painted faces and swinging axes.

Further back in the ranks, the knights in their bright orderly rows wavered with barely contained impatience. The horses whinnied nervously, smelling blood on the wind. Then at last the signal to attack was given. As one, the knights raised their whips and struck the flanks of their mounts, urging them into furious motion.

"Strike down the monkeys!"

"For Captain Leegan!"

"Mongaul! Mongaul!"

With loud cries the armored cavalry advanced, led by the blue knights and the aged Count Marus. Behind them came the black knights under the command of Irrim and Tangard, and finally, the red knights, led by Astrias. The white knights remained in a strong formation surrounding the lady general's flag behind the center of the battle lines. From the perspective of this central command, the three knightly orders that were now advancing seemed like rivers of color, rushing toward the chaos of the fight as if to sweep away the swirling melee of footsoldiers and wildling warriors. It was a dazzling sight, both the riders and their armored mounts gleaming so brightly in the morning sun that they were painful to the eye. Riding tall, the knights drew their sparkling longswords and crashed into the battle lines. Fiercely the riders lashed out on every side, sending Sem heads flying where they struck.

Yet the Sem, too, had grown accustomed to this kind of combat, and they put their past lessons to deadly use. Far more agile than the heavily armored knights, they sought to dodge under the wide arcs of the cavalry's swords and launched themselves at the horses' legs, cutting and jabbing, all the while shrieking their high-pitched war cries. If this tactic failed, some worked in pairs to attack the mounted knights from above, one Sem acting as a platform from which the other leaped high with ax or dagger swinging. Others thrust poisoned stone spears up at the horses' bellies, or clambered onto stirrups and saddles where they clung like fleas, swiftly jabbing with their poisoned spears at the knights' faces and throats.

As they had in all the previous encounters, the Sem made up for their inferiority in numbers, strength, and weapons by capitalizing on their tremendous speed and agility, making this an even fight. The Mongauli were warriors trained for battle in the green Middle Country, where sturdy protection was more often important than speed. Here, the heavy armor and helms that they wore restricted their movements; with their faceplates lowered, their vision, too, was restricted, and they remained vulnerable to strikes that pierced their throats and armpits or attacks that hamstrung their steeds. Their horses were not well suited to running across the drifting sands, which sucked at their hooves and made them stumble whenever they sought to turn. Moreover, few among the human fighters had the reflexes to respond to the darting quickness of the Sem warriors.

Atop their rearing chargers, the knights thrashed like cattle trying to beat off pestering flies with their tails. On the firm, open terrain of their homeland, or on broad city streets where they could gallop freely, they could have cut down a force of un-horsed attackers almost at will, or better yet, used swords and lances like proper knights against another force of cavalry. That was battle! But this killing of nimble wildings was aggravating and difficult, and their tactics were ill suited for the work.

Unable to fall back on their training, they sought to use their much greater strength to the utmost against their foes. Many a Sem warrior leapt upon a mounted knight only to be shaken off and thrown to the ground, there to be trampled by the churning hooves of the warhorses. And when the Mongauli longswords struck home, they could split the skulls of the Sem with ease, scattering blood and brains across the battlefield. Many of the knights adopted a sweeping sideways stroke, as though they were cutting wheat back in the autumn fields of their homeland; this way they could attack several Sem at once, and those who were not quick enough to jump over the flashing blades or duck low beneath them would be cut entirely in half and sent tumbling grue-somely, their shrill voices shrieking and failing. But the Sem rarely stayed in one place long enough for the swords to hit their mark, and so the battle raged on, neither side gaining a clear advantage.

"Aiii! Kweeeh! Yiiaaah!" the cries of the Sem filled the air with indecipherable insults and curses.

Marus scowled at the noise. The old count was right in the midst of the attack, maintaining his position at the head of his blue knights. His blue captain's plume waved above the cavalry vanguard as he cut through the fray, moving no slower than many of the younger knights. Garanth rode close to his side as one of his flag bearers, guarding the count without pause.

From time to time as the melee eddied around him Marus would withdraw his beloved blade, drenched in wildling gore, and pull back behind his flagbearers to rest for a moment and look over the battle. There was chaos on all sides, spraying blood and flying sand, horses rearing and wildings swarming so thickly that it was hard to tell one from the other.

Once, the severed head of a Sem flew up into the air, trailing a red gout of blood across the men below, a grimace of hatred frozen on its painted face. This brought a round of cheers from the invaders, but the sound was soon lost beneath the frantic whinnying of horses and screams of men as two steeds were brought down by Sem spears and collapsed on the crimson sand, throwing their riders to be trampled under the wildling horde.

"Hmm," Marus grumbled as he surveyed the scene, easing his thirst with a flask of water handed to him by one of the knights of his guard. Just a few yards away the battle raged. His men were fighting with their faceplates lowered, knocking aside the poisoned spears that were thrust at the weak armor at their necks, trying to hold the line against a determined Sem advance. Their shining blue armor was stained with the blood of friend and foe.

"Hah! Foul monkeys!" Marus heard a voice exclaim behind him. "By Istar, they're fiendish, smelly brutes!"

The voice was familiar, young and lively; it came from the tall rider who now rode swiftly past the count, swinging his sword with determined ferocity, cutting down Sem to right and left. His skill was impressive. The count's hard-set eyes softened. "Eru. You'll not die here, either," he muttered softly. Garanth, by his side, gave no sign that he had heard the count. Silently the lieutenant raised his faceplate and took a gulp of water.

"How many youths have perished under these flags," Marus continued, too low for even Garanth to hear, "on the streets of Parros during the War of the Black Dragon, and now here, painting the wastes of Nospherus with their blood—for Mongaul, for Mongaul..." The count's eyes were filled with deep sadness. "For Mongaul," he repeated. "I understand why we fight. I know it is our destiny to rule this land. But I do not want to see another young man fall. Not one." He shook his head and gazed out toward the front lines once more. Eru of Argon was gone. Like a galloping thunderbolt he had disappeared into the melee, cutting as he went.

I am getting old, thought Marus, then he cleared his throat and turned to his lieutenant. "Back into the fray, Garanth."

"Ready, Lord Captain," said Garanth, slapping his chest in a firm salute, which Marus knew meant: *I am old, but I can fight harder than any younger man.*

Marus waited for him to lower his faceplate and then shouted "For Mongaul!" and charged toward the turmoil of the lines, sword swinging.

"For Mongaul!!"

The shout went up on every side, the men answering their captain.

Astrias, accompanied by his lieutenant, Pollak, sweltered back in the rearguard. He regarded his placement in today's formation as a clear sign that the lady general's dissatisfaction with him had not yet abated. When it came time for a retreat, or should they need to about-face and attack an enemy from behind, the position of rearguard could be one of great honor, but not today. Today they were to meet the enemy head-on, and chase them head-on should they withdraw. Only the most useless of captains would have been assigned to the rearguard today.

And now the battle was joined and playing out a good distance from his position, so far that he could barely hear the courageous shouts of his fellow knights taking enemy heads. Astrias's mood grew darker.

He should be up there with them, winning victory—and winning her heart.

Although he had not yet fully realized it, Astrias was very much enamored of the Lady General Amnelis, she of the shining golden hair and cool emerald eyes. She made him want to achieve great things, to win her praise—and, just maybe, her smile of satisfaction. But from the very beginning of this excursion all his efforts had gone awry. First he had failed to capture Guin and the four other fugitives, leading most of his strike force to bloody death in the Nospherus interior... And then, when he tried to make up for his failure by chasing down the Sem without waiting for the lady's orders, the vanguard he urged on had fallen into the yidoh trap and Captain Leegan had perished. Both times he had escaped while others died. Both times he had come back defeated, ashamed of his failure, ashamed to be alive.

If I had only been given the front lines this time, I would be washing off that shame, finding a way to make this disgrace right again.

But instead of giving Astrias a chance to redeem himself, his liege had scorned and scolded him harshly, throwing him in the rearguard. Just thinking about it set a fire in Astrias's breast.

Everything is his fault! His fault! Guin...

Just mouthing the name in silence was enough to make his heart tremble with hate so hot it nearly drove him mad. Guin, that leopard-headed freak, was the one who had shamed him, had made his beloved goddess look upon him with cold eyes. He was the one who had brought Astrias so low. One more mistake and the young knight—once admired by all as the Red Lion of Gohra—would lose his post as captain. Amnelis had said as much.

The thing that stoked the fires of his shame the highest was that the strange warrior had not even taken him seriously when he had challenged the fiend to single combat.

You are no challenge for me, little one. Wait twenty years and come again. Then I will fight you.

He knew Guin had been laughing at him behind that leopard mask—a cold, harsh laughter, not of victory, but of pity! Thinking on that moment, Astrias felt his shame burn white-hot, casting tall shadows of anger.

And now I've been told to wait in the back, where I've not a chance of taking one enemy head, not one!

All Astrias could hope for was the impossible—a sneak attack from behind, led by Guin himself.

I'll show him my mettle when next we meet! If only I am given the chance...

The young captain had been thinking of nothing else for a while now. From time to time he rose in his saddle, scanning the fray far ahead of him for a sight of the leopard-man towering above the clashing armies. Unable to spot his nemesis, he felt uneasy at first, wondering where the terrible warrior might be and what he might be planning. His unease changed to elation as he considered the possibility that Guin might indeed appear behind the army and answer his misguided wishes.

Come out, Guin-fiend! Then we'll see who's the little one! I challenge you, Guin!

"Captain!" Pollak called out as though he'd read Astrias's mind. "I wonder what's going on. I don't see that leopard-head anywhere."

Astrias started, then assumed an air of nonchalance. "Perhaps he's leading another party around to the back."

"I would wish nothing else," Pollak replied. He knew well what it was that his captain truly desired. "Then we'll hunt that freak ourselves. Captain."

"What?"

"Who do you think he is, sir?"

"A good question."

"Where did he come from? You would think we would have heard if such a warrior lived among us in the Middle Country."

"He might just be someone we know. Someone famous."

Astrias thought back on the discussion at the war council three days before.

"I wonder what we'd see if we took off that mask."

"Indeed." Astrias seemed suddenly uncomfortable talking about his adversary, but Pollak continued, unaware of his captain's mood.

"What is he thinking, anyhow—a man, taking the wildling Sem as his allies? Indeed I cannot believe that the royal house of Parros has actually joined forces with these desert barbarians. I saw the spires of Crystal. It was a beautiful place. Every Parrosian I saw was beautiful, too, all fair and slender, with skin as white as alabaster."

Astrias said nothing. He was thinking of someone more beautiful still, but these thoughts were madness, and certainly nothing he could share with another, not even his trusted lieutenant.

"The royal family of Parros and the Sem—it's impossible," Pollak declared with finality. Then he laughed harshly. "But these are all things we can find out once we capture the leopard-man and persuade him to spit out what he knows. Captain? Are you listening?"

"Huh? Ah, what?" Astrias turned, pretending that he had been surveying the battle.

"In any case," Pollak added, "it is our utmost priority to do whatever we must to take the leopard-man, and bring him before the lady general. Or bring his head, at least."

"Absolutely." Astrias smiled with the thought. Then his tone changed as he gazed out toward the front lines again. "Ah, Pollak."

The other looked, hearing the anger in his captain's voice.

"Look, they're doing it again. The Sem are pulling back again." Then Astrias slapped his saddle and swore. The Sem didn't ever want this battle to end, obviously. They had had their fun and now they were retreating, again.

Dom dom dom dom dom dom...

The wildling war drums beat a quick rhythm, mingling with the screeching war cries of the Sem as they turned and ran back up the dunes en masse, without discernable order or pattern.

This time, however, the knights of Mongaul were not of a mind to let them leave.

"Wait, you cowards!"

"We won't let you escape this time, monkeys!"

"We'll wipe them out! Follow them! Follow!"

"Begin pursuit!"

"Orders! Orders! Pursue the Sem!"

Today, the Mongauli army was a mighty arrow loosed from a ready bow. There was no turning back, no slowing down. They had waited far too long to let this opportunity pass.

"Garanth!" Marus wheeled his horse around to join his lieutenant in the line of blue knights that was quickly reforming at the base of the dune.

"My lord!"

"After them!"

Count Marus waved the baton in his hand and quickly the blue knights of Tauride showed the quality of their training, spreading rapidly into five lines for the pursuit.

"After Marus Corps! Forward!"

In an instant, the desert was transformed into a dry riverbed along which a four-colored flood of men and horses readied to pour in haste.

"Doalspit!" Astrias swore far behind them and reluctantly formed up the men of his rearguard. Then the blue, the black, the white and, lastly, the red knights of Mongaul shouted their battle cries and began to move forward, chasing the retreating Sem up the face of the dune. The battle for Nospherus was entering its final act.

"Chase them! Chase them!"

"Beat them into the sand!"

"Leave none alive!"

"Mongaul! Mongaul!"

The wildlings ran so fast that they became furry streaks across the sand, fleeing from the Mongauli army, racing away from the surging multicolored mass of the Gohran cavalry like prey taking flight before a swarm of yidoh. The horses spat foam through bared teeth, their manes and tails flying in the wind. The knights, eager to prove themselves in battle, set in with their whips to urge their steeds to even greater speed, quickly pulling ahead of the charging footmen.

The horses' hooves dug into the sand, kicking up a spray of dust hard on the heels of the fleeing Sem. Seeing their foes in full retreat, both the knights and their mounts were consumed with the wild fervor of the victorious. Their bloodshot eyes flickered with eagerness and they shouted and howled sounds that were not words. One thought drove the ten thousand-strong Mongauli army after their enemies: that today, here on the desert sands, all accounts would be settled. Their burning bloodlust drove away all fatigue and all fear of the cursed desert and the monsters that lay hidden beneath its surface.

"Aii! Aiiie!"

"Alphetto!"

The Sem ran as fast as their legs would carry them, their haphazard ranks dissolving even further in their mad rush to escape the unexpected Mongauli onslaught. Whether or not they had noticed the lift in the Mongauli's morale after their attack began, it would have been too late then for them to change their strategy, and now they could do nothing but run for their lives. But their feet were swift—they were said to be among the quickest runners of all the desert's creatures—and they soon put distance between themselves and the heavily armored pursuers, whose horses' hooves sank deep into the sand.

Seeing their quarry pull away, the Mongauli became desperate.

"Orders! Orders!"

Their white shoulder tassels flowing, Amnelis's messengers sped until their mounts were nearly spent, catching up to the hindmost riders of the blue knights at the front of the formation. "From the General of the Right to Captain Marus, orders! Orders! Marus Corps is to pursue the Sem!"

"Surely she did not expect us to do otherwise?" Garanth shouted, his voice hoarse with desert grit. "Blue knights, onward! To victory and glory!"

Like a gleaming blue wave the knights of Marus Corps rose high in their saddles, their courage a visible swell, their whips and swords held firmly in their hands. Count Marus glanced quickly backwards. Trailing off behind his formation were the two thousand black knights of Tangard; they were already a considerable distance behind his own riders. And yet the Sem were pulling away from Marus's men.

Charging over the crest of a dune, the pursuers were surprised to see that not far ahead, the flatness of Nospherus was marred by a series of low rocky hills. The dark crags thrust up through the sand so abruptly that they seemed like an afterthought added out of mischief by some creator-god. Here and there between the dunes over which they now rode and the hills that lay ahead, the knights could see rocks half-buried in the desert, some round like boulders and others flat and dark like sheets of frozen sand.

The gentle yet deceivingly high roll of the dunes had hidden the rocks and the jagged hills until now. It was clear that the hills were the destination for which the Sem were making.

Marus drew back on his reins and shouted out loudly above the drumming hooves. "Men! They intend to run for those crags. We must not allow them to reach them, or they will be able to ambush us at will. Don't let the Sem get into the hills!"

The knights under Marus's command gave a shout and once more lay on with their whips and dug in with their spurs, urging on their exhausted mounts. They rode so hard they nearly flew out of their saddles, leaning so far forward that they were close to falling over the necks of their horses. They gripped their swords so tightly with their mail gauntlets that it seemed their fingers would cut through the very leather of the hilts.

Neither Marus nor his followers paused to wonder why they had not seen the leopard-headed Guin today—he who had ridden with the Sem on every raid until now. They had little time to consider anything in the midst of their pursuit, as they moved with the force of a tidal wave across the desert; and, unlike the unfortunate Astrias, none of Marus Corps had ever crossed swords with Guin personally, nor had they exchanged words with the warrior or felt his incredible presence make their skin crawl and the hairs at the backs of their necks stand on end; and so, they lacked the young captain's obsession with their mightiest enemy. Moreover, had they taken note of Guin's absence, it would soon have slipped from their minds again, its oddness disregarded, so preoccupied were they with the fury of the chase.

The obvious danger posed by the leopard-man's absence was that he might be leading another strike force around to attack the Gohrans from the rear. But that could be left to the rearguard Astrias, or to Irrim should the young Lion of Gohra fail. The main concern of the blue knights now was to keep the Sem from reaching the hills that lay ahead. With hardly a glance to either side, they charged on after their foes.

The front of the Sem line disappeared around another, lower dune, heading straight for the rocky hills that seemed somehow much closer now. The hills were the kind of rocky wasteland crags that could only be found in Nospherus, gray and bare, without a single tree or blade of grass to color their slopes. Although they were not tall, they were divided into many layered strata, with numerous canyons running into their depths. If the Sem took refuge there, it would surely take the Mongauli a long time to root them out.

In hot pursuit, the blue knights of Count Marus rounded the dune not far behind the wildlings. Tangard Corps, well behind, chose a different route, trying to save time by racing up and over the dune face. The black knights pounded over the ridge of sand, giving a cheer when they saw that they had gained on their quarry. But as they galloped down into the hollow on the far side, the ground shook—and split beneath them!

"Aaah!"

Men screamed as their horses' hooves trod air.

"Stop! It's a trap! A pit!"

Within moments the sandy hollow was echoing with the cries of knights and horses as they struggled wildly in the bottom of an enormous pit that had opened up suddenly underneath the foremost riders.

Unnoticed in the shadow of the dunes, two small groups of Sem now took cover, discarding the severed ends of bristly vine ropes that they had carried from the oasis. The ropes had served their purpose, for they had allowed the Sem to rig a concealing layer of flat stones over the recently abandoned pit of a mouth-of-the-desert. When cut, the ropes had in an instant released the stones and the sand that hid them, sending the knights and their mounts crashing down into the pit.

Trying to stay upright atop their flailing horses, the leading black knights dropped down with them into the gaping hole. Even at the edges of the pit, the sand was far too soft to give the charging horses any traction, and many of those who stopped before they fell in ended up sliding down nonetheless.

"Halt! All halt!"

The warnings and shouts shot back toward the oncoming remainder of Tangard's men, punctuated by the panicked whinnying of the horses, the yells of the latest riders to tumble into the trap, and the death-cries of the first to fall, now being crushed by those who had followed them.

"Help!"

"The pain! I can't move!"

"Agh! My leg... My leg!"

The pit trap filled quickly with an impossibly tangled mass of desperate men and horses weighed down by their splendid but brutally heavy armor. As they struggled, the white sand flowed in around them with a dreadful rush of sound. In moments, those lowest down were completely buried, their screams and cries for help abruptly silenced.

"Halt! All halt, it's a trap! A Sem trap!"

Finally, Irrim's shouting got through to his men, and the remainder of the black halted their charge.

Irrim's messengers relayed the orders back down the line. Confusion reigned among the rearmost soldiers, who did not realize what had happened. They milled about angrily, unwilling to miss their chance to carry out the long awaited final slaughter of the Sem.

"What? Why stop? We've gotten no such orders!"

"Marus Corps has already gone ahead! What's the matter? Why do we have to stop?"

"Were we not commanded to pursue them to the end?"

"What's going on? What happened up at the front? More yidoh?"

"What? What is it? I can't see anything!"

"Stop! Stop! Stop!"

Nearer the pit, in the bustling hornet's nest of men and horses, Irrim shouted for his friend and fellow captain from atop his horse. "Tangard! Tangard! Are you okay?" He grabbed one of the men who had stopped just in time to avoid being dragged in with the rest. "Has Tangard fallen into the pit?"

The man shook his head uncertainly. "I do not know, sir…"

"Captain! Captain!"

The black knights from Talos Keep circled around the pit, desperately trying to save the screaming wounded and their horses from the sandy morass. It was a race against time. Like a fire spreading through dry brush, the Doal-sent sand flowed ceaselessly in from all sides, threatening to bury every horse and man alive and leave the hollow as flat and featureless as it had seemed moments before. Numerous troops were already lost beneath the smothering cascade.

"Captain Tangard!"

"Captain!"

The men around the pit called out desperately for their leader. Then a dying horse rolled away from the center of the pit, and they saw him. Tangard had been right in the middle of the formation and had fallen toward the top of the deep pile. But when the knights spotted their captain, half buried in the tangled bodies, his bearded face was pale and his eyes were shut. He did not seem to be trying to push his way out, nor did he reach for the outstretched hands of his men.

"Lord Captain! Lord Captain! Here, my hand!"

"Tangard! Are you wounded? Tangard!"

Irrim, his closest friend, with whom he had led the black at Talos Keep for many years, leapt down from his horse, pushing through the men who stood at the edge of the pit. Quickly he and several others grabbed the unconscious Tangard's hands and pulled him from the mass of bodies, freeing him from the weight of a horse that had fallen against him. But when they lifted him up towards the edge of the pit...

"Tangard!" Irrim shouted.

Several of the men around him exclaimed in horror. When the fallen horse had crashed into the captain, one of its iron stirrups had pushed through a chink in his black armor, its sharp tip cutting deep into his abdomen. Pulling him away from the horse had tugged the stirrup loose, but at the same time it had torn open a bloody wound in his side. His guts were spilling out and steaming in the dry air.

"By Janos! What ill fortune is this?" Irrim wailed, pale as Tangard himself. Some of the men around him choked back vomit.

Tangard moaned weakly, and Irrim turned to shout to the riders atop the dune. "He's still breathing. Medicine! Bring bandages!"

Several of the other knights yelled frantically for the medical squad. Irrim hugged his friend to his breast and pressed his hand to the wound, trying to stop the flow of blood, staring in shock at the red tide gushing out between his fingers and onto his legs.

Then in an instant the tragedy was laid aside as a new cry went up from the men who were further from the pit.

"Ambush!"

"The Sem!"

A hail of black Sem poison arrows descended suddenly upon the knights from both sides, sending some for cover and knocking others down into the pit to die with their comrades.

"Fiends!" Irrim grit his teeth and roared. "Foul Sem! You will rue the day you stood against the Mongauli black!"

"Attack! Attack!"

In these close quarters, with no room to charge, the knights' horses were of little use; nor of any help were the crossbowmen who had just come hurrying up from behind. Pinned down by the rain of arrows, the knights used their horses as shields, or lowered their faceplates and lashed out blindly at the throng of oncoming Sem.

Arriving with her guard at the top of the dune, Amnelis gazed down on the hellhole below, her ears assailed by screams and sobbing moans. Not wishing to leave the wounded as they were, the lady general sent out orders for a squad of white knights to aid in the rescue of the fallen, but the area around the pit, where the casualties were worst, had already become a milling chaos of Sem and black knights, with horses galloping wildly and footsoldiers darting back and forth. Going in there meant meeting the poison arrows and stone axes of the Sem head-on.

Amnelis went pale with rage, gripping her baton with hands that trembled in anger. In the hollow below, the shifting white sand continued to sift down, burying the living and the dead alike, while into its gaping maw more bodies fell one after the other.

Meanwhile, unaware of the fearsome death they had narrowly avoided, Marus Corps galloped onward. Having gone wide around the dune and the trap it hid, they had left Tangard Corps far behind as they pursued the fleeing Sem. Marus, with his lieutenant Garanth directly to his rear, galloped midway along the advancing columns of horsemen.

Suddenly the blue knights heard a commotion far behind them and the whooshing sound of sand. This was followed an instant later by a cacophony of screams.

"The Sem!"

"An ambush!"

"Lord Captain!" Garanth urged his horse alongside that of Marus. "Lord Captain!"

"I heard." The count turned in his saddle and looked back.

The smooth white face of the nearest dune blocked their view, but the sounds of clanging metal and the high-pitched war cries that they could hear now coming from the other side were unmistakably those of battle. These were sounds with which they were by now all too familiar.

"There must have been a unit waiting in ambush," Marus said. He kept his horse galloping at a steady pace. "Those Sem are crafty, but I smell the leopard-man's hand in this. He is too clever, that one."

"Well," said Garanth, sounding worried. "What will we do, Lord Captain?"

"What will we do?" Marus shot him a disparaging look. "There are eight thousand men in our main force, and the Sem, without those—" Marus jutted his jaw forward, indicating the Sem that still ran ahead of them towards the mountains, "they surely don't have ten thousand warriors to spare for an ambush. There is no cause for concern."

"Then we continue our pursuit?"

"Of course." Marus glared after the retreating Sem. "Leave

the ambushers to the rest of our men. They've got Tangard, Irrim, and young Astrias back there. Those Sem won't even slow them down. We will do as we have been ordered and run these Sem into the sand!"

Garanth grinned.

"Yes," Marus continued, "we've come too far to let them get away into the hills where they can hide and ambush to their heart's desire. I'm sure they wouldn't lead us straight to their villages, but if we keep chasing, and keep chasing, they'll eventually run out of places to hide. Then we will crush them. I'm sure the rest of our army will have joined us by then."

"Understood!" Garanth's sunburnt face smiled. Then he dug his heels into his horse's flanks and pulled ahead, shouting as he rode up the line, "Keep chasing! Do not fall behind! We'll take their nest this time!"

Marus glanced back once more, looking for some sign of the rest of the army, but it seemed that the fight was still going on, as none of Tangard's men had yet cleared the dune.

The hills ahead were nearer now, and seemed larger. The galloping knights could see a path leading into a narrow valley that curved around the skirts of the nearest crags and then plunged between them. The foremost of the retreating Sem had just reached the entrance to the valley.

"Don't let them escape!" Garanth raised his voice over the

pounding of the horses' hooves. "Don't let them into the mountains! We're on rocky ground, watch where you ride!"

The Mongauli knights whooped in response. They were elated. The ground had gotten harder and their horses no longer sank into the sand. At last, they were picking up speed. They raised their whips, trying to urge the last bit of strength out of their frothing, exhausted mounts.

"Chase them! Chase them!"

"Run them down!"

"For Mongaul!"

The lead knights quickly closed the distance between them and the Sem stragglers.

"Hraah!"

From atop his horse, one of the knights swung down his sword in a great arc that terminated at the bobbing head of a fleeing Sem. The wildling's skull split down the middle, sending up a fountain of blood.

Talented as the Sem were at running across the desert, on hard ground their speed could not compare to that of the horses. On the rocky slope below the hills, the blue knights gained rapidly on their quarry. Within moments they were among the fleeing Sem, and they slashed out to right and left with their swords, cutting down wildlings with each stroke.

Some of the Sem stopped and fought back, swinging their

axes wildly, or leaping past the knights' swords to grab onto their legs, trying to pull the Mongauli off their horses. But this scattered resistance did little to slow the swift cavalry. One after another the struggling wildlings were flung into the air by the charging horses, and most of those who survived the impact were cut in two before they could pick up their weapons and defend themselves.

A few of the Sem were able to leap high enough to evade the oncoming chargers, but the knights beat them down with blade, hilt and pommel, quickly dislodging the few who managed to gain a hold on the horses' backs. Flailing to regain their balance, the repulsed Sem tumbled down the horses' sides, and were cruelly slashed by the knights' spurs as they went. The chargers galloped on, trailing crimson lines across the white rocks behind them. The bodies of the wildlings fell to the ground and were trampled by succeeding knights.

"Aiiii!"

"Alphetto!"

The screams of the wildlings were filled with fear. The entrance to the dry valley had become the scene of a massacre.

The Sem have no strong leader, other than that leopard-man. They're primitives, a race of monkeys. Before they can even think to regroup and strike back they have already fled onward in fear.

Marus paid little attention to the Sem who were running on both sides of him. He kept his gaze firmly forward, and kept his horse moving. Garanth had left his side to race further ahead, and held his sword raised, brandishing it at the fleeing Sem. This was no contest of strength between proud wildling warriors and the sturdy knights of Mongaul. This was a monkey hunt, a scouring of screeching animals by men that were now killing partly for the fun of it.

Unease had been growing for a long time in the old count's heart, and now it spread and wrapped around him like angel hair blowing softly in the wind. But when he tried to divine its source, the unease melted just like angel hair, leaving no trace. Behind his faceplate, Marus furrowed his white brows, and sighed. *How dark my mind has become! But what use is this worry, this baseless gloom?* He shook his head and spurred on his horse.

"Don't become preoccupied with hunting down your quarry!" he shouted to his knights. "Leave the difficult ones be, we are here to find their villages and strike at their very root! We will wipe the Sem from Nospherus soon. This need not be the final battle. Save your strength!" Despite his age his voice betrayed no frailty as he rode through the midst of the harrowing scene.

The white valley was stained red with blood. Furry limbs and severed heads were scattered across the stony ground, intermixed with dismembered torsos and looping strings of guts. Moans, screams, and death rattles mixed together, and the cheers of the victorious Mongauli knights rose above all. More and more small furred bodies were pummeled under the horses' hooves, or cut in two by the Mongauli swords; wildling heads, their eyes white and staring and their teeth locked in fierce final grimaces, flew high in the air, trailing blood under them and landing with wet thumps on the valley floor.

The sight did little to stir the old, battle-weary count. Taking care that his horse did not slide on the blood, Marus rode through the hell, his tassel flowing behind his blue cloak and helm.

"Lord Captain! Lord Captain!"

A knight, gasping for breath, rode toward him from up ahead.

"What is it?"

"Lord Captain, you are here!" said the knight, short of breath. "We've won! We've won! The Sem village—"

"What?" Marus stood up straight in his saddle. "What of the Sem village?"

"I've found it! It lies just ahead!" The knight raised his hand and pointed back in the direction from which he had come. His mailed hand was trembling with excitement.

"What?! Are you sure?" Marus exclaimed.

"Yes, I am certain. They were trying to run into their village. It's at the bottom of this valley."

Marus half-turned as if to shout back to the rest of his force, then paused and looked at the knight again. "Who are you? Raise your faceplate. If what you say is true, you're in for a major distinction."

"It is true, by the green fields of Mos, I swear it!"

The knight's voice was full of fervor. He raised his hand and lifted his faceplate. Marus smiled a broad smile.

"Eru of Argon!"

"M'lord!"

The youth's eyes shone like fiery opals. His face was taut and his breathing hard as he smiled victoriously at the count.

"You have done well!" Marus was on the verge of appointing him head of his guard right then and there. After a moment's consideration, he decided that this was better done later; there was no time to lose now. "Down that valley, you say?"

"Yes, m'lord."

"Excellent. Garanth! Garanth!"

A few moments later Garanth was riding rapidly among the troops, giving hurried orders. The blue knights promptly ceased their slaying of the few Sem in the valley who remained to oppose them. "We ride on the Sem village! Leave no one alive!

Spare no woman or child!"

The other officers took up the call. "Take no captives! Kill them all!"

"For Mongaul! Mongaul!"

The shouts of the knights echoed through the valley, followed by the sound of their horses' hooves, pounding like an earthquake.

"Mongaul! Mongaul!"

Marus swung back his cloak.

"Eru! Lead us!"

"As you command."

"To the Sem village!"

Like a blue tidal wave of death, the two thousand knights galloped through the hills, shaking the ground of Nospherus.

—— 4 ——

"The village of the Sem!"

It was closer than the invaders had thought.

Surprised by the ease with which they had discovered their goal, the Mongauli soldiers erupted with shouts of glee.

The village that lay before them was a simple affair, a collection of huts looking like upturned bowls made of white, hardened mud. The structures stood clustered along a dry streambed that ran through the center of the valley. In the middle of the space they sheltered was a small clear area, perhaps a gathering place. Thin wisps of purple smoke rose from some of the huts as though the Sem who lived there had just kindled their cook fires to prepare a meal. Several stakes had been driven into the dry streambed, upon which were hung the skins of some animal—and round dangling objects that the Mongauli soon realized were the heads of men hung out to dry in the hot Nospherus sun.

Not a single wildling was in sight.

Perhaps the quickest of the Sem who had fled before the blue knights' charge had run into the village and raised the alarm, warning their wives and children of the coming danger, and the tiny barbarians had abandoned their belongings and rushed from the village in haste. Or perhaps the furry primitives had simply panicked and run inside their huts, where even now they sat clinging to each other in abject fear, mother holding child, elder holding grandchild, sister holding sister, silently invoking the name of their monkey god, fearing the coming of the devils in their gleaming iron skins atop their giant four-legged beasts.

Or...

Marus slowly raised his faceplate. His alert eyes scanned the village, looking for clues, hints that might indicate what had become of the Sem that lived here. Instinct told him that they were not in those huts.

"Garanth."

"My lord?"

"This is a large village," Marus spoke softly. The rustling of the sand in the soft wind had all but stopped. This could be a valley of death—a ghost village—it was so quiet. The wildling shelters sat still and sullen between the valley walls, and not a single hairy body strewing the path that the Mongauli had come could offer any information.

The oppressive silence was soft as cotton, but as stifling as a yidoh's insidious clutch, enveloping the knights in its gigantic veil. Tension spread through the mounted riders. They stilled their breath. Someone toward the back of the line let his hand drop slightly, inadvertently striking his sword against his armor and giving off a loud metallic clang. Several knights gasped and held their breath.

But nothing happened, and the silence stole back in like Nospherus sand that sifts to fill a hole in the desert and obscures all that has gone before. Nothing stirred within the quiet huts; there was no movement in the streambed. The riders stared at the severed heads hanging in the sun, as though their swollen lips might part to tell them where the villagers had gone, but the heads, too, were silent.

"Captain..." Garanth uttered, his voice heavy, as though he had just stepped into the hallowed Temple of Janos and feared to break some edict of silence. He brought his horse up along-side Marus's steed but paused hesitantly, unsure of how to continue. Marus turned and looked at him, reflecting on the busy decades during which this man had ridden by his side—his old subject, his confidant, his friend. Their age was the same, and ever since they first stepped onto the field of war at the age of fifteen, they had witnessed every battle together. Neither man had ever been seriously wounded; through all the grueling campaigns they had managed to avoid sword, mace, and arrow, and the crippling falls from horseback that had claimed so many former companions. In Parros, Cylon, Terelle-Alam, and finally stationed at Tauride Castle...

As Garanth rode up alongside the count, a sense of security filled Marus, and the old friendship that had matured over long years of reliance and loyalty welled up in his warrior's heart. They had known each other when their hair was blond and their beards were first growing; now their hair was as white as snow. He did not want to see that friendship ever die.

How far we have come...

"Captain?"

Marus awoke from his reverie with a start. This was no time for reminiscing. He had just opened his mouth to give Garanth his orders when a sudden yell cut through the silence of the valley.

"Hraaah!"

The entire corps started, as jarred as if they had missed a step while walking down a staircase; some almost lost their balance and fell from their horses. One of their number had inexplicably broken ranks and was now riding straight down into the village at a furious speed.

Marus was aghast. "What is this? No one moves without my orders!"

Garanth gaped, dumbstruck for a moment before he recovered enough to yell for the rider to stop. But the knight rode on, leaning so hard over his horse that he nearly toppled from his saddle. He was galloping down into the valley as though his life depended on it.

"Garanth!" Marus looked around at him and nodded.

Garanth gave the signal to attack, his arm tracing a swift arc through the air, and a moment later the cavalry was in motion. With a sound like rolling thunder, the blue knights of Mongaul charged down into the Sem village.

Marus's eyes opened wide and he shouted out to Garanth as they galloped. "Was that Eru who raced ahead?"

It was, the aged count thought. *It was Eru of Argon. Trying to prove himself, that youthful fool. Even if only women and children are left, this is a Sem village and we've fallen prey to their traps before. Who knows what they might have planned?*

Yet even as he cursed Eru's foolhardiness, he saw that the young knight had made it through the middle of the village without mishap and was now riding up the slope at the other side of the valley.

"What is he doing?" Marus demanded, pulling on his reins. The rest of the blue knights had reached the first of the huts and they were slowing down, moving more cautiously now.

As Marus watched, Eru rode still farther away from the corps, up onto the rise that overlooked the far side of the village.

Then he lifted his hand and lowered it sharply.

At his signal, the valley began to growl and shudder around the Mongauli riders. The very ground beneath them shook as the sound rose to an incredible roar. For a moment, they had no idea what was happening. When they did realize, it was already too late. From the tops of the high hill-walls on every side, an avalanche of boulders came rolling down into the valley.

The soldiers screamed.

With inescapable speed, the boulders spun down the valley's sides, as though spit from the mouth of a volcano, bouncing off the rocky slopes and crashing down on top of the knights. The Mongauli's iron helms and armor could do little in the face of such destructive force, and the men were crushed as though they were made of paper, flattened beneath the rampaging rocks. In a matter of seconds, the valley that had been so silent was filled with screams of pain and shrill cries for help.

When the dancing dust that had been thrown up by the boulders as they careened off one another began to settle down, those who remained of the proud blue knights of Mongaul could see that their mighty corps had been transformed into a sorry band of cursing and crying wounded men. They lifted their dimming eyes and peered through the turmoil, and they saw them, hundreds of little devil faces gazing down from among the rocks atop the valley walls.

They were the faces of the Karoi—the first that had been seen by the Mongauli since they crossed the Kes—but to the knights below, they were indistinguishable from those of any of the other wildlings. They were evil and monkeylike, to be hated and feared.

The huts in the valley where the blue knights now found themselves were Karoi homes; this was their village. When word of the invaders first reached them, they alone of the Sem had been unwilling to march to war. But when the news arrived from the Sem gathered at the oasis that the Mongauli army was searching for their villages, that indeed they were drawing closer to their rocky hills, they had sent out scouts. The few that returned had confirmed what the other Sem had told them, and they had realized that they had no choice but to join the fight.

Gaulo, the leader of the Karoi, had put aside his past differences with Loto, Tubai, and Ilateli, and in an impassioned meeting at the oasis the night before Guin left to find the Lagon, he had agreed to join them in the struggle against the *oh-mu*. Guin had needed a force of Sem to prepare an ambush, and Gaulo had volunteered the Karoi. It was his Karoi warriors who now looked down from atop the cliffs, awaiting the signal to attack. Gaulo, perched at the head of the valley, made a swift pushing motion with his arm. With a roar, a second wave of boulders came rolling down mercilessly upon the heads of the Mongauli.

"Watch out! Lord Captain, get down!"

Garanth sprang from the saddle and grabbed his captain by the leg, dragging him off his horse and pushing him behind a heavy boulder that had lodged against the ruins of one of the Sem huts. He hoped that the stone and the horses standing in front of it would be enough to shield them from this new on-slaught.

They had been lucky to escape the first avalanche, but it seemed unlikely that their luck would hold. The sound of huge rocks rumbling and cracking against each other drowned out the screams and laments of the knights. All around them the simple hardened mud huts of the Karoi were crushed to pieces as the stones thudded and rolled across the valley floor.

"Lower your head! Get down!" screamed Garanth. Marus was in a daze, seeming not to understand what was happening to them.

"Eru, what have you done?" muttered Marus. He tried to stand and search for the errant knight as though he was back at camp surveying his ranks, as though no giant boulders were rushing down upon his force to reduce his men to bloody gore.

"Lord Captain, it's a trap! We've fallen into—"

Garanth's voice was suddenly cut off.

Marus turned just in time to see a boulder slam into his loyal lieutenant's face. The count gasped and came to his senses.

"Garanth! Garanth!" he shouted, running toward his friend. Garanth lay sprawled on the ground, his feet facing away from Marus. Where his head should have been, a giant white boulder had come to rest, giving the perversely comic illusion that his white hair had suddenly ballooned to an enormous size.

"Garanth!" Marus shouted as though his words could shatter the stone, then threw himself against the great rock, pushing it aside. But as it rolled away he staggered back, aghast. Where Garanth's head had been, there now remained no more than a sticky gelatinous paste of stony white, gray, and red.

"Garanth!" Marus screamed so hard he could taste blood in his mouth. He looked up and down the valley, his face wild. It seemed that the Sem had prepared in a hurry, for they were already out of rocks—at least, no more were falling. The valley floor was strewn chaotically with those that they had already pushed down. More than half of the once proud blue knights of Tauride Castle were dead. They lay scattered, crushed and broken, some now nothing more than pitiful lumps of blood and flesh.

Of those who had not been killed outright, many were pinned or trapped by the larger stones, and their moaning and the pained whinnying of their horses filled Marus's ears. It was a few moments before he realized that the loudest and most piercing of the screams was his own.

He fell quiet then, gazing up to the top of the nearest valley wall and the countless furry faces of the Sem. The wildlings were colored with warrior's paint, and they now held up their bows above their heads and cried their piercing war cries.

Then Marus saw him: a tall man in the armor of Mongaul, below the Sem, halfway down the valley wall.

"E-ruuuu!"

A cry, barely human, came from Marus's grimacing mouth. He could clearly see the lone knight's long blue cloak, his blue armor—knight's armor, bearing the crest of Mongaul—the longsword at his waist, and his long blue leather boots. Eru lifted a mailed hand and slowly took off his helm, topped with the crest of Tauride Castle; he threw it down among the rocks with casual disdain.

The face that was now revealed was fine-featured, dusky, and burned by the sun. *He is so young*, the count thought, and he did not see that the young knight's features were taut and trembling. The obsidian eyes, usually filled with humor and a cold cynicism, were open wide, and they seemed about to overflow with barely contained emotion. His mouth trembled—he was biting his lower lip hard—and his hand clutched at the edge of his cloak. He could not spot Marus down below until the old count slowly took off his own helm, revealing his white hair.

Istavan of Valachia lifted a trembling hand and brought it swiftly down.

"Kiiiiyaa!"

"Iiiie Iiiie!"

Almost dancing with excitement, the Karoi scampered down the valley side, passing Istavan where he stood watching. They came in threes, each group carrying a large urn between them. When they drew near the bottom of the slope, they upturned the urns and poured their contents down onto the valley floor.

"Wh-What is this?"

The survivors of Marus Corps, wedged between boulders, or holding onto the wounded and the dead, peered warily at the liquid being poured down on them. They all feared the black poison of the Sem, but this was clear and odorous.

A horrified shout rose up from the knights.

"Oil!"

"Cactus oil!"

"Those Sem mean to burn us alive!"

"Janos protect us!"

"They wouldn't. They wouldn't..."

Yet already a unit of Sem that had been lying in wait had appeared at the top of the cliff, bearing arrows with flaming tips in their hands. They blazed like a row of torches at a funeral procession.

For a moment Marus's face, white as paper, was drawn tight. In the next moment, his features twisted and crumbled with the weariness of utter defeat. A hoarse voice spilled out from his loose lips.

"You...you schemed? You wore the armor of Mongaul...of Mongaul...and chanted its name, and yet...and yet, *this*?"

Count Marus summoned the last of his strength and rose to his feet, leaning on his sword as if it were a cane.

"You traitor—you *rat!* Eru of Argon!"

The count reeled. His vision narrowed suddenly, as if he were staring into a burning spyglass. No longer could he see his men dying around him, or the Sem at the top of the cliff, or the flaming arrows that the wildlings held ready to fire, or the immanent disaster that awaited him. Only one thing filled his gaze, and it was the young knight Eru—Istavan of Valachia—standing above him on the valley side.

"You will pay dearly for this. You... Even if my body is crushed, I will avenge Garanth!"

Suddenly, with amazing speed, the count drew back his hand and flung his sword like a spear toward Istavan. It was an incredible throw, higher and farther than even a champion could have hoped to hurl such a weapon. Istavan yelped and dodged aside, but he could not avoid the streaking blade entirely. It cut into his right ear, sending out a spray of fresh blood.

"Yaaah!" the mercenary howled, clapping his hand to the wound. He raised his other hand in anger and shouted, "Now! Do it!"

"Iiiiaaah!" screamed the Sem archers, and they loosed their blazing volley into the sky. Within moments the valley of the Karoi was engulfed in flames.

The fire ignited the flowing cactus oil and swept wildly toward the Mongauli troops and their horses at the bottom of the valley, charring them like meat in a frying pan as it rushed over them. Quickly the flame spread, burning hotter off the fat of man and horse. Those who were not caught immediately by the conflagration ran madly looking for a way out, but the Sem had filled in every path out of the valley with their boulders, and several wildlings now stood at each blocked exit waiting for the men to try to climb out. Shouting victoriously, they rolled down more rocks now from on high and shot at the panicked knights with their poison arrows. When the fire showed signs of weakening, the Sem women hurried up with more urns and added more cactus oil to the blaze to ensure that its fury did not diminish.

The valley became a roaring sea of fire, a rock-filled crematorium where the Mongauli burned alive. Blackened like the shades of the damned, the knights jumped and jerked in a dance of death, stumbling blindly back and forth while the cruel flaming tongue of Migel Firegod licked them until they were dead.

Yet in the middle of that blazing hell, Marus still lived. Oil stained his body, and the fire had reached his feet; it had swallowed the blackened corpses of his men all around him, and now it licked hungrily at the noble captain. Already, the edge of his cloak was smoldering, but still he stood tall on that killing ground.

His white hair flew upwards in the heat, and his face was painted red by the light of the blaze, as though he were Migel himself, come to pass judgment in the court of Hell. His bloodshot eyes never wavered, following Istavan as he retreated from the fearsome pyre toward the top of the cliff.

Stricken by a sudden power he did not understand, Istavan froze. He was exhausted, and the heat was unbearable. He knew that he had to get to the top of the valley wall; yet, he turned around. He was cursed. He could not take his eyes off of Marus.

Then, with a swift noise like that of a rushing wind the flame consumed the body of the count. It was as if the old warrior had been gently bestowed a kiss of fire by the air maiden Aeno, or lifted away to a higher plane by the swooping fire-chariot of Ruah Sungod. Surrendering his body to the flames, Marus stood until his white hair burned. His blue armor turned red hot as he was transformed into a giant human torch.

Just as he was about to disappear into the flame forever, the count's eyes opened wide.

"Eru of Argon!"

The eerie voice reached Istavan at the top of the cliff. It seemed to echo throughout the valley, louder than even the maelstrom of fire below.

"Eru of Argon! Mongaul will never forget your name, you rat! Eru of Argon! Eru of Argon... Eru..."

Just when Istavan was about to cover his ears and scream "I'm not Eru!" the count's body collapsed backward into the deadly flames without another sound. Hardly a thing moved in the valley, then. Only the fire continued its feasting without pause.

Istavan's face was pale.

"Please," he spluttered. "Please forgive me. It wasn't my idea, the oil... Guin thought of this! By the head of Cirenos he wears, if you're going to curse someone, make it him, not me!"

Then, as though trying to shed his assumed identity before the curse could find him, he frantically yanked off the blue armor of Tauride Castle that he wore and threw it into the fire. His eyes were filled with tears.

It was some time later when the remainder of the Mongauli army, having finally dealt with the ambush at the pit-trap, made it to the valley where Marus Corps had met its fate. They had seen the smoke rising and had hurried as swiftly as they could. When they arrived at last, it was only to realize that they were far too late. The Sem had vanished, and their warriors and village-folk were nowhere to be seen. All that the invaders found in the valley, lying among the boulders and broken mud huts, were the sad remains of Tauride's corps of blue knights, charred as dark as despair, caught forever in twisted shapes of pain.

Guin's plan had worked beautifully.

END OF BOOK FOUR

Coming in July 2008

THE GUIN SAGA, BOOK FIVE:
The Marches King

by KAORU KURIMOTO

Paperback
288 pages
5.5 x 7.5 inches
$9.95/$11.95

Though devastated, the Mongauli army finally regains its game in inhospitable Nospherus with Guin absent from the Sem ranks. While the leopard-man has found the Lagon, securing their aid proves easier said than done.
Stirring finale of the "Marches Episode."

Get Volume One Now!

THE GUIN SAGA *Manga*
The Seven Magi

ILLUSTRATED BY
KAZUAKI YANAGISAWA
STORY BY
KAORU KURIMOTO

Paperback, 172 pages
6 x 8 inches, $12.95/$17.95

Many years after awaking in the Roodwood, the leopard-headed warrior has become King of Cheironia. Only he can dispel the black plague that ravishes his realm.
A three-volume manga based on the first *gaiden* side story of the saga. Ages 16 and up.